William Gilbert

**The Inquisitor**

Or, the struggle in Ferrara. An historical romance. Vol. 1

William Gilbert

**The Inquisitor**
*Or, the struggle in Ferrara. An historical romance. Vol. 1*

ISBN/EAN: 9783337065782

Printed in Europe, USA, Canada, Australia, Japan

Cover: Foto ©Andreas Hilbeck / pixelio.de

More available books at **www.hansebooks.com**

# THE INQUISITOR

OR,

## THE STRUGGLE IN FERRARA.

### An Historical Romance.

BY

## W. GILBERT,

AUTHOR OF "SHIRLEY HALL ASYLUM," "DOCTOR AUSTIN'S GUESTS,"
"DE PROFUNDIS," ETC.

IN THREE VOLUMES.

VOL. I.

LONDON:

TINSLEY BROTHERS, 18, CATHERINE STREET, STRAND.

1870.

LONDON :

SAVILL, EDWARDS AND CO., PRINTERS, CHANDOS STREET,
COVENT GARDEN.

# CONTENTS

OF

# THE FIRST VOLUME.

———

# THE INQUISITOR;

OR,

## THE STRUGGLE IN FERRARA.

———

## CHAPTER I.

### THE MONK.

ON a calm evening in the month of
May, 1554, a man in the dress of a
Capuchin Friar, having a half-filled
wallet slung over his shoulder and a stout
staff in his hand, wended his way towards
Ferrara. Although he was still several
miles from the city, he was evidently exhausted, and appeared to continue his
journey with much difficulty. He would
frequently stop to rest for a few moments,
and then apparently summoning up fresh
courage, continue his way for some distance,

and then rest again. Beyond the fact that he was somewhat above the middle height, it would have been difficult to judge of his appearance, for although the weather was sultry and oppressive, he wore his cowl so far forward on his head as almost entirely to conceal his features. This was evidently done purposely, for the sun was already so near the horizon that he had nothing to fear from its rays; and had he studied his personal comfort, he would naturally have thrown his cowl back on his shoulders. To have formed a tolerably correct opinion of his age would have been as difficult as to have judged of his features. True, he stooped considerably in his walk, and his pace was slow and deliberate, but these might rather have been occasioned by exhaustion and fatigue than by the weight of years; and this supposition was still farther increased by the accumulation of dust on his sandalled feet and on the edge of his frock.

As he journeyed onwards a singular peculiarity was observable in the Friar. As a rule, his order was habitually most communicative, entering willingly into conversation with all who addressed them ; and as they were generally looked upon as the newsmongers of the country districts, few passed them without exchanging at least some sentences. With our Friar, on the contrary, this was far from being the case; and he appeared to avoid, as much as possible, the peasants he met, taking care to pass them on the opposite side of the road, and returning with courteous, though few words, the remarks they made when they had reached him.

Night began to set in, and stars, one by one, to shine forth in the heavens, while myriads of fireflies illuminated the fields by the side of the road, flashing their lovely light with such brilliancy as almost to dazzle the eye. The calm beauty of the Italian sunset, however, appeared to have no charms for the wayfarer, and he continued on his road till he had nearly reached Mal-Albergo, situated on the banks of the river, nearly opposite to the principal gates of Ferrara, when the sound of the church bells calling the congregations together for the benediction, warned him that he had nearly arrived at his journey's end. But instead of hurrying on to secure a place in the last ferry-boat, he suddenly stopped short, and seating himself on the bank by the road-side, appeared to meditate deeply, as if undetermined what course to pursue, evidently wishing to reach the termination of his journey, yet for some strong cause hesitating to enter the city.

He remained for some time seated, alternately glancing at the lights which began to appear in the city as night advanced, and then on the road and country around him, as if anxious to meet with some person to whom he could apply for information. No one, however, appeared; and he rose from his seat, and turning his cowl back on his shoulders, proceeded onwards for a few paces, when he again suddenly stopped, and retraced for some distance his steps, looking eagerly on each side of the road, as if trying to distinguish whether there might be any habitation near. At last he saw a light in a meadow at a little distance from the road. He was on the point of proceeding to it, when he suddenly halted, as if to determine what the light might be, for it appeared to be too close on the ground and too bright to be in any dwelling. The idea then struck him that it might merely be a will-o'-the-wisp hanging over the marshes, as was common at that season in the districts around Ferrara; but a moment's thought told him that this could not be so, as the colour was too red.

He now hesitated no longer. Leaping from the bank, he approached the light, though with some difficulty, his steps being impeded by the brushwood, and his feet

clogged by the swampy nature of the soil.
Still he pushed onward, and at last came
close to the light, which he found to proceed from four torches tied together, their
shafts stuck into the ground. At first he
was greatly puzzled how to act, as he saw
no one near, nor could he divine for what
purpose the torches had been placed there;
but at length he perceived a man some ten
or twelve yards from the light, seated on a
stone, his elbows on his knees, and his face
buried in his hands.

The Friar again drew his cowl over his
head, and, without hesitation, walked up to
the man, and said softly to him—

"My son, are you asleep?"

"I am not; but had I been, I should
hardly have thanked you for waking me,"
was the uncourteous reply of the man, who
still remained in the same position, with
his face buried in his hands.

"I am sorry to disturb you," said the
Friar, "but you would greatly oblige me by

telling me if there is a ferryman anywhere near who could row me over to the city."

"The only ferryman near here," replied the man, without raising his head, "is the one at Mai-Albergo; but I suspect you will be too late for him, as he must have left off work half an hour since."

"But I did not wish to enter the city by the Strada del Po, and I had a dim recollection that there was another ferry farther up the river."

"You are a stranger, then?" said the man, still maintaining the same position.

"Not altogether," said the Capuchin. "I have visited Ferrara more than once already; but the last occasion was several years ago."

"It must be a strong temptation that induces you to return to it again," said the man, sardonically. "It is the last place in the world I should wish to visit, if I could once get clear out of it."

"Still that is hardly an answer to my

inquiry. I asked you if I could find a ferry-boat farther up the river; and if you are able to answer the question, you would greatly oblige me by doing so."

"There is another ferry-boat about half a mile farther on," said the man; "but you will find some difficulty in reaching it through the swamps; and then, again, you will not get Giacomo, the ferryman, to leave his bed at this time of night without being well paid for it. I know him too well for that."

"That is unfortunate for one of my order," said the Friar; "for we rarely carry money with us, and I have none."

The man here raised his head for a moment and gazed at the Friar with much curiosity and evident interest. Then rising from his seat, and taking off his cap, he said, in a tone of respect which strongly contrasted with the abrupt manner in which he had hitherto replied to the Friar's inquiries—

"Ah! pardon me, Reverend Father, I did not know to whom I was speaking, or I should not have been so uncivil. What can I do to serve you?"

"Thanks, my son," said the Friar; "all I wish is to enter the city by the Porta San Giorgio. Can you assist me in doing so, by telling me in what manner I can cross the river, for I tell you candidly I have no money to pay the ferryman?"

"And I am sure Giacomo, who is little better than a pig of a heretic and an imp of Calvin himself, would rather go without his money than row you over, monk as you are, even if you could pay him. But he will soon have his reward; the times are now fast changing; the heretics have had their day, and now ours is coming."

The Friar, from under his cowl, examined his companion minutely, lit up as he was by the burning torches. He was an old man, about seventy years of age, with low forehead, deep sunk, sparkling black eyes, indicative of great cunning, and sickly, swarthy, sallow complexion. His dress, which was that of the poorer class, was covered with mud, with which his feet and hands were also begrimed. Altogether he was of most repulsive appearance. His demeanour to the Friar was now, however, most respectful, and even courteous.

"You seem to take the behaviour of your friend Giacomo much to heart," said the Friar; "but can you tell me of any other way by which I could cross the river?"

"Wait one moment, Reverend Father," said the man; and then advancing towards the torches, and examining a sort of leather trap, something like a long wide-mouthed bag, which had been placed on the ground before the light, but in which he found nothing, he said, with an expression of anger on his countenance—

"It's all useless, all in vain; nothing seems to prosper. I believe the anger of heaven is directed against the city and all

the country around it. It's no use my remaining longer here ; and it's better for me
to be in my bed, than run the risk of
catching the plague in these marshes."

Then, taking up the leather-bag, and
throwing it over his shoulder, he snatched
up the torches, and throwing them on the
ground, extinguished the flame, leaving
himself and the Friar with no more light
than was afforded by the fireflies sparkling
around them.

"Reverend Father," he then continued,
" I will row you across the river myself, for
I have a boat fastened to the shore, a few
hundred yards from here ; and then, as you
say you are almost a stranger, I will accompany you to the gate of San Giorgio, and
put you in your way to the Capuchin convent, where, I suppose, you will lodge for
the night. It will be better for me to accompany you than Giacomo, even if you
could get him to leave his bed."

" Why so ?"

" Because, as I told you before, Giacomo is a heretic, and every one he ferries over is examined at the gates, and a hundred questions asked, such as, with whom they are acquainted in the city? what their business is there? how long they intend stopping? and many other inquiries of the same sort. Now, with me it is different. I am known as a good Catholic, who would no more bring a heretic into the city than the plague itself."

The Friar made no reply to the man's observation, but thanked him warmly for his offer of assistance, and the two started off towards the river.

" You observed, my son," said the Friar, " that you might as well be in bed as run the risk of catching the plague in these marshes? Do I understand you to mean that the plague is again in Ferrara?"

"Well, I cannot state for a certainty that it is," said the man; " but several cases very like it have already been sent to the

Lazaretto. But that it will come, there can be little doubt; and terrible indeed will it be when it does come."

" What makes you think so, my son ?"

" Because heaven, in its anger at the favour shown to heretics, has already withdrawn from us all means of curing the plague; and when it comes we shall have to submit to it without help."

" Don't you take too gloomy a view of the case ?" said the Friar.

"Certainly not," replied the man. " Who knows better than I do ? Have I not been there where you found me night after night, burning my torches, which cost me three soldi a piece, without any return, leaving me a loss both of time and money ?"

" But I don't understand in what way that proves that it would be useless to adopt any remedies against the plague. What were you seeking for ?"

" Seeking for !" replied the man somewhat angrily. " Why, for the only secure remedy but one against the plague—vipers, to be sure! Here I have been night after night trying to catch them, and, as I said before, burning my torches to no purpose, and have not caught three in a week. In the days of the last Duke, I have frequently known ten to be caught in a night, and once my son-in-law caught as many as nineteen. Then, again, no more scorpions are to be found in Bologna, and without scorpions and vipers how will it be possible to cure the plague-stricken? I speak from experience. When the plague was in Ferrara, about the time of the marriage of the Duchess Renée—evil befall her!—we had abundance of vipers, and many were cured of the plague; but now we shall be utterly at its mercy, and bound hand and foot when it comes."

"But why do you say, 'Evil befall the Duchess Renée,' my son?" asked the Friar. "What has she done to offend you?"

"Offend me!" replied the man. "Has

she not offended the whole country, and heaven itself, by introducing into Ferrara the swarm of heretics who came in her train? And has Ferrara ever flourished since? No! I know it better than any one, for everything has gone wrong with me since I first saw her face. I had then a good appointment, which I had held for years, giving perfect satisfaction to every one, but before she had been here three years I lost it."

" But was the loss of your appointment caused by any fault of the Duchess Renée?"

" Certainly it was. For twenty years I had turned the hands of the clock in the Rigobello tower, but some heretic French or Swiss, who came with her, proposed that the hands of the clock should be moved by wheels, weights, and ropes, and the old Duke Alfonso, her father-in-law, who was always too fond of new ideas, agreed to it. Two years afterwards all was completed, and after twenty years' service I was discharged."

"But, after all, it appears to me that, if you have any complaint, it should be against the old Duke Alfonso and not the Duchess Renée, as she seems to have had nothing to do with the alteration."

"Nothing to do with it!" said the old man, testily. "If she had not come here at all, the man who proposed the alteration would not have been in her train, and a good Catholic—sinner as I am—would not have been thrown out of bread by a foreign heretic."

"But surely you do not mean to say that, after so many years' service, you were dismissed without compensation? That seems hardly to correspond with the character I have heard of Duke Alfonso, who appears to have behaved liberally and honourably to all."

"I don't wish to say anything against the old Duke, who was in every respect an

excellent Prince, and very kind to every
one, as long as they didn't offend him; but
if they did, they might as well have asked
mercy of a hungry lion as of him. However, it's true, when they sent me away,
they gave me ten scudi and an appointment
in the Lazaretto; but although the pay-
ment was equally good I didn't like the
occupation. There was nothing regular
about it. It's a very difficult thing for a
man who has been accustomed for twenty
years to do nothing else than turn the
hands of a clock to get out of the regular
habits and notions he has acquired."

"Still, I do not see how that could have
interfered with your duties in the Lazaretto.
Did they not keep regular hours there?"

"Nothing could be more irregular. The
sick would come in at all hours, and some-
times two or three together; then perhaps
we should have none for a day, and afterwards a rush of half-a-dozen at a time.
Then some took their medicine at one hour

and some at another; till at last I told Dr. Castagna that I must leave the establishment, or I should certainly go out of my mind.    He replied that he had great pleasure in granting my request, and that I might go as soon as I pleased."

" And what did you do afterwards?"

" Well, I applied for the situation of bellringer at the cathedral, and obtained it, but I soon gave it up."

" Why was that?" said the Friar.   " I should have thought the regularity of the hours of the service would have been agreeable to you."

" So I expected, but it was far from being the case."

" Why so?"

" Well, the hours of service were all regular enough, and for a day or two all went on swimmingly, but then I began to have conscientious scruples whether I could continue it with safety to my soul, so I gave up the appointment."

"But what possible scruples of conscience could you have had in such an appointment? I should have thought it difficult to have found a situation more suited to your taste and capacity."

"It would have suited me perfectly well had it not been for one circumstance. The Archbishop had ordered that the services were to be regulated by the new-fashioned clock in the Rigobello tower. Now, as the machinery moving the clock had been made by a foreign heretic, it went against my conscience that the services in the Cathedral should be regulated by it."

"I think, my son, you were a little too scrupulous on the occasion," replied the Friar; "but at the same time are you quite sure personal feeling had not something to do with the matter? I mean, your labours being regulated in some degree by the clock of which you no longer had the control."

" Possibly that might have had something to do with it, Reverend Father."

" And what occupation did you afterwards take up?"

" I went back to the Lazaretto, and again induced them to give me some employment ; but I got tired of the irregularity of the hours, and left a second time.    Then I offered myself as an assistant to Bruno, the executioner ; but he said I was too old and weak for his work."

" You surely do not mean to say you would have accepted a situation under the common executioner?" said the Friar, with marked disgust in his tone. " At your time of life, you might have sought for some other employment, no matter how humble."

" Don't think ill of me, Reverend Father," said the old man. " Bruno is not the common executioner. He only applies the torture and punishments to the prisoners in the dungeons of the Inquisition, and executes those who are condemned to death for heresy. I would never have helped the town hangman at the execution of a thief or a murderer. No; I'm not so low as that."

" Is your friend Bruno much occupied at present?" inquired the Friar after a moment's silence.

" Every day in one way or another, but principally in the prisons of the Inquisition. We have not had many public executions for heresy lately ; not more than four in the last fortnight. The Duke is away, and the Duchess has more of her own will than she would have if he were here. After all, she would be a brave woman were she not a heretic. Why, they say that Father Pelletario, the Duke's confessor, is positively more afraid of her than all the heretics in Geneva put together. But we are now at the river-side, and here is my boat. Get into it, and I will ferry you across."

Little conversation passed between the Friar and his companion during their passage across the river. Arrived at the other side, the old man fastened his boat to a post by the side of the water, and he and the Friar proceeded to the gate of San Giorgio.

"Can you tell me," said the Friar to his companion, "whether the Duchess is at present in Ferrara?"

"She is," replied the man. "She is living at the palace of San Francesco, where she has a court of her own. They say the Duke and she are not friends. I hope it's the case, though of course I know nothing as to the truth of the statement. This, however, is certain, that when he is in Ferrara (he is now at his hunting seat at Belriguardo, they say) he lives in the Este palace while she is at the Palace of San Francesco."

"But why should you be glad of a misunderstanding existing between the Duke and his wife?"

"Because I hate her, and the whole foreign troop with her."

"Did she ever do you any personal harm?"

"No, nor to anyone else that I know of; but she has tried to do a great deal of harm to their souls."

"In what way?" asked the Friar.

"By pretending to do a great deal of good to the poor and needy, helping them in every way that she can. Trying first of all to gain their love, for the purpose of handing them over to the enemy of mankind, whose agent I believe her to be."

"My son," said the Friar, "let me advise you to speak a little more cautiously. Remember that walls have ears, and the Duchess is still a powerful princess."

"Her time is coming though, and will soon be here," said the old man. "But I'm astonished, Reverend Father, to hear you talk in her praise."

"I merely speak in your interest, my son," said the Friar mildly. "Even if there should be a disagreement between the Duke and his wife, depend upon it he would punish you for speaking disrespectfully of the Duchess. With me of course it will go no farther, but let me advise you not to speak in that way before others."

"You're right, Reverend Father," said the old man after a moment's reflection. "Thank you for the hint."

"I understand, then," said the Friar after a short silence, "that you live in Ferrara?"

"I do," replied the old man, "and have lived in it since I was a child; and with the exception of the time when I was pressed as a soldier and made to join the army under the late Duke Alfonso, I have never been ten miles from it in my life. To say the truth, my experience on that occasion gave me little wish to roam. Night after night did I sleep on the damp field, or stand sentry on the river's bank to watch for the approach of the Venetians. Hardships enough I then endured. I had little to eat,

no praise, and small pay. If I did my duty
I was ordered to do more; if I attempted to
avoid it, my captain flogged me. To end
the matter, I was wounded in the last fight
and almost lost my life, and from that time
to this I have never had any inclination to
leave the city for more than a mile or two
at a time."

"Of course you are well acquainted, then,
with Ferrara?"

"No man better. I think I know every
house in it, and every man, woman and
child, that is to say, by sight, of course, for
I haven't much to say to those above me."

"Perhaps you can tell me, then, if the
Count Biagio Rosetti,—I mean the chief of
the twelve Judges,—is in Ferrara at present?"

"He is, Reverend Father; I saw him in
court this morning when I went to hear the
trial of a friend of mine who had been
accused of robbing a Jew. It was an unfortunate thing for him that the Judge

Rosetti presided in the court, otherwise I'm sure my friend would have escaped."

" How so ?"

" Because, being a Lutheran himself, the judge naturally favours all schismatics, infidels, and idolators, and instead of dismissing the case he sentenced poor Beppo to be soundly flogged, as if to steal from a Jew was as bad as to rob a Christian."

They had now arrived at the gate of San Giorgio, when, to the Friar's dismay, he found it closed.

" Do not annoy yourself," said the old man, " I know the porter. He is a good Catholic, and will let one wearing your frock into the city without difficulty. I will speak to him and all will go well."

The man now proceeded to the wicket gate, and knocking at it requested that it might be opened, saying, that he had with him a Reverend Friar who was going to the convent of San Maurelio, but had been delayed on his road. The porter without hesitation opened the gate, and the Friar and the old man entered.

" And now, Reverend Father, I am near my lodging. Continue your road straight onward, and you will find your convent in the first street to the left."

The Friar thanked the man for his courtesy, but instead of entering the street as directed, he turned round to see whether he was followed, and finding, after waiting a few moments, that no one approached him, he passed the street leading to the convent, and continued his road till he reached the Via della Piopponi. For some time after having entered the street he examined carefully the houses on each side, as if in search of one, but uncertain which it might be. Even after he had twice passed the whole length of the street he appeared undecided, and remained for several minutes in the centre of the road, waiting for some one to approach who might be able to give him the information he required. Presently he saw by the light of the moon, which had now risen, a young man leave the archway of one of the best houses in the street; and to him he determined to apply for information. Rapidly hurrying after him, he said,

"Pardon me, my son, for interrupting you, but could you tell me the house of the Count Biagio Rosetti, the chief of the twelve judges?"

"It is but a few steps farther back," replied the young man. "It is the one I just left. Shall I conduct you to it?"

"There is no occasion, my son. I noticed the house when you left it. It is that with a light in the window of the room over the archway."

"It is," said the youth. "But you had better let me conduct you; the staircase is dark and dangerous, and I am sure the Judge would be very angry with me, if, after I knew you wished to visit him, I allowed you to run any danger by letting you find your way alone."

"Do you know the judge intimately, then?" inquired the Friar.

"Without vanity I may say I do," was the young man's reply. "He was my professor when I commenced my legal studies in Ferrara, and I have been intimate with him for more than three years."

"Are you an Italian?" asked the Friar.

"Why do you ask, Reverend Father?" said the young man, with some reserve. "You must either be unacquainted with Ferrara, or you must know that we are not accustomed here to answer questions that every stranger may put to us, without fully understanding his object."

"I should have thought, my son, that my habit alone would have been sufficient guarantee that I intended no harm."

"Hardly, Reverend Father," said the young man. "You know our saying, 'The cowl does not make the monk;' and if the proverb is true anywhere, it is certainly so in Ferrara."

"I meant no offence, my son," said the Friar. "My only reason for asking the question was, that you, while speaking Italian perfectly, appear to have a slight foreign accent."

"Possibly you expect I may be a Frenchman, or from Geneva," answered the youth, "and as such, probably of the same religion as the Duchess?"

"Once more, my son, I intended no offence. Why should you speak to me in the manner you do? You have kindly pointed out to me the house I was searching for, and I need trouble you no further."

"True, Reverend Father. Still, I am a free agent in the matter, and would prefer returning with you. If you are really a Friar, as your dress appears to indicate, so warm a professor of the reformed doctrines as the Judge might like to have a witness on his side of the conversation which passes between you. If he finds my presence unnecessary or inconvenient, of course I shall

leave immediately. But of this I am determined, if you persist in your visit, I shall
return with you."

The Friar hesitated for some minutes,
as if in doubt what steps to take. At last
he said to the youth, "Are you also a fol-
lower of Calvin or Luther?"

"Again, Reverend Father, I must remind
you it is not our habit in Ferrara to make a
confident of the first comer, however
respectable his appearance may be. You
must see yourself, that were I a protestant
and therefore in danger of persecution for
my religious opinions, a Capuchin Friar is
hardly the person I should choose to confide
my secret to. Once more, will you allow
me to be your guide to the Judge's rooms?
And let me add, that if you intend to visit
him to night you must decide quickly, or
he will have retired to bed."

"I thank you for your offer, my son, and
will follow you," said the Friar.

The youth now returned to the house he

had quitted, and on reaching the gateway he took the Friar's hand, to lead him up the dark staircase, which with considerable difficulty they contrived to ascend, proving the truth of the youth's statement, that the Friar would find a guide necessary. On arriving at the first floor the young man knocked at the door, and in a few moments footsteps were heard approaching it.

" Who is there?" inquired a voice from the inside.

" Good friends," was the reply. " It is I, Camille Gurdon. On leaving your house I was overtaken by a Capuchin Friar, who was seeking you, but did not know your abode, and I have brought him with me."

" Before I open the door I must know his errand, and who he is."

" I will explain who I am to your full satisfaction, my son," said the Friar, " if you will allow me to enter. What have you to fear from me? I am an old man, older than yourself, and besides that you

have the support of the youth who has so
kindly accompanied me to your house. For
mercy's sake do not hesitate, but allow me
to enter, for I am sick at heart, and my
strength is utterly exhausted."

"But, Reverend Father," said the voice
behind the door, "if you are a Capuchin
Friar, what business can you have with me?
Why should you ask hospitality of me
when you have your own convent, one of the
richest in Ferrara, to receive you? Do you
know me?"

"Perfectly well," said the Friar, "although it is now some years since I saw
you."

"Tell me your name."

"I cannot, before a stranger. But why do
you hesitate to allow me to enter? As I
said before, I am old and powerless, and
you have nothing to fear. This I promise
you, if you will allow me a moment's interview, and you then desire me to leave your
house, I will do so immediately, even

though I should die of exhaustion before your door."

After a few moments' silence on both sides, the door was opened by a venerable looking old man, in a velvet robe, with a black skull-cap on his head, and holding a lighted lamp in his hand. Surveying the Friar with great curiosity not unmingled with impatience, he said to him—

"Reverend Father, if you will neither tell me who you are, nor allow me to see your face, I must request you will immediately leave my house. I am but a bad guesser of riddles, and have no taste for mummery. Once more, let me know who you are, or begone."

The Friar advanced a few steps, and when in such a position that his youthful companion could not see his action, he raised his cowl sufficiently to allow the Judge to see his features, and then instantly replaced it. A marked change now came over the behaviour of the Judge to his visitor, and with much friendliness in his tone, he asked him to enter, and preceded him to the sitting-room, while the youth remained without to re-fasten the door. As soon as they had entered the room the Friar whispered to the Judge—

"Can you not dispense with the presence of that young man, as I wish to speak with you alone?"

"Just as you please," replied the Judge; "but you have nothing to fear from him. A stauncher adherent to our cause, Ferrara does not hold."

"If you know him," said the Friar, "1 make no further objection. At the same time, I would rather speak with you alone. Were it only my own secret I had to keep, I should not mind his remaining, but I am intrusted with those of others as well."

"I will immediately dismiss him then," said the Judge. Then addressing the young man, who was now entering the room, he continued: "Camille, my son, you can leave us, as my friend wishes for some private conversation with me. We shall meet again to-morrow."

The young man bowed submissively to the Judge's remark, and after wishing him good evening, unbolted the door and quitted the house, leaving the Judge and the Capuchin Friar to continue their conversation undisturbed.

# CHAPTER II.

## BERNARDINO OCHINO.

E must here, for a few pages, stay
the current of our narrative, to
introduce more particularly to the
reader the mysterious monk—Bernardino
Ochino. Of the many champions of Protestantism in Italy, few among them had
laboured more zealously, or had done better
service in the cause of truth, than he.
Nature seemed to have especially endowed
him both mentally and physically for the
fatigues and dangers he had undertaken.
In person he was somewhat above the
middle height, strongly though not heavily
formed, and altogether having a frame
capable of enduring a vast amount of

fatigue. His face was eminently handsome, even at the time of our narrative, when he was considerably more than sixty years of age. In fact, when he was younger it would have been difficult to have found an individual possessing a more expressive countenance. Nor was the classical shape of his features the sole recommendation of his face—it beamed with intelligence and candour. Perhaps the most singular characteristic in his countenance was the extraordinary combination it displayed of mildness and determination. Nor was the expression an untruthful one; for while gentle to all, and anxious to avoid giving the slightest offence to any, yet no danger was sufficiently terrible to make him quit a labour he had once considered it a duty to his Maker to undertake.

Bernardino Ochino was born in the year 1487, at Sienna, in Tuscany, of obscure parents, and when young had been educated for the law; but being of a pious turn of

mind, he determined to relinquish the legal
profession and enter the Church. It is not
known at what ecclesiastical seminary he
prosecuted his studies, but after his ordina-
tion he appears to have joined the Franciscan
Observantines, who were considered the
strictest of all the orders of the regular clergy.
In this order he continued for many years,
gaining great popularity as a preacher.
But rigid as the rules of the Observantines
were, they were not sufficiently so for Bernardino, and he quitted them to enter as a
simple friar the order of the Capuchins.
Shortly after he had joined this new brotherhood, and long before he had fully adopted
the Reformed principles, he began to turn his
attention to the abuses which then existed
in the Church, and he attacked with great
severity the luxury and effeminacy of the
priesthood. Had he commenced this attack
some thirty years before, it is more than
probable he would have been quickly
silenced; but so weakened had the Church

of Rome become by its own corruptions,
that its heads readily perceived that if some
reformation did not take place in the habits
and manners of the clergy, it would be impossible to check the advance of the Reformed doctrines; and Bernardino, instead
of being silenced and discouraged, was not
only protected by the College of Cardinals,
but though still a simple friar was raised to
the dignity of Confessor to the Pope himself.
No monk perhaps ever had greater power in
his hands, or exercised it with more modesty
than Ochino. Riches and honour both
appeared utterly indifferent to him, and he
continued to advance in the goodwill of
every one.*

By his own order, especially, Bernardino
was greatly admired and beloved. Long
after he had (in their estimation) degraded
them by adopting heretical opinions, the
annalist of their order speaking of him says,

---

* See Note, page 45.

" In such estimation was he held, that he
was esteemed incomparably the best preacher
in Italy, and his powers of oratory and
graceful action all powerfully enlisted the
sympathy of his audience, and this the
more so as the admirable tenor of his private
life corresponded so perfectly with his doctrines." Although a favoured guest in the
palaces of princes and nobles, he never rode
on horseback or in a carriage, but performed
all his journeys on foot. Nor did he relinquish this habit even when far advanced in
years. In the pulpit, he was admired by
all; in fact, in such estimation were his
sermons held that, when he preached in the
immense Cathedrals of Ferrara and Modena,
even standing-room could not be found for
all those who wished to hear him. The
Emperor Charles V., who when in Italy was
a constant attendant at his sermons, said of
him, " How great is the power of that man !
he would make the very stones weep if they
could hear him." Sadolet and Bembo, who

were far better judges of oratory than his
Majesty, admitted Ochino to be the most
eloquent preacher of his day. In the year
1538, Ochino was chosen General of the
Order of the Capuchins, and, as a proof of
the extraordinary respect he was held in,
he was again, in another chapter, held at
Whitsuntide, 1541, and in direct opposition
to his own wishes, re-elected General of the
Order, a mark of respect which had never
yet been shown to one of its brotherhood.

So great was the fame which Bernardino
Ochino had acquired as a preacher, that he
was specially sent on a mission to those
centres of Italian heresy, Ferrara and
Modena, to counteract the march of Protestantism, which had already gained an
immense number of converts. Although
Ochino entered into his work with great
energy and zeal, the natural honesty of his
disposition would not allow him to shut his
eyes to the abuses existing among the
clergy of those two cities; and while

preaching eloquently the doctrines of the
Church of Rome, he took occasion at the
same time to lash most severely the corruptions which had been introduced among its
clergy. But Ochino, in his attacks upon
Protestantism, being actuated rather by
an erroneous conception of the truth than
any personal animosity to the Protestant
professors, attempted by argument to convince them of their danger. In this, however,
he signally failed. He entered into discussions and arguments with Peter Martyr, of
Vermigli, and into correspondence with
Calvin, on what he considered their heretical doctrines. Tradition even says, that
on more than one occasion he met the great
leader of the Protestant faith in Italy, in
the apartments of the Duchess Renée,
where the arguments were carried on with
great animation but perfect courtesy on
both sides.

The results of these discussions were such
as greatly to diminish the faith of Ochino in

the doctrines of the Church of Rome. Being convinced of his errors in many points, he acknowledged them, both in private and in the pulpit, to the great dissatisfaction of the Archbishop and clergy, who strongly remonstrated with him on his conduct. Ochino, however, was not a man, when once convinced, to allow any power to bias him, and he continued his preaching, which day by day began to assume more of a Protestant tendency, till at last, to the great dismay of the Catholic clergy, he openly declared himself a Reformer. Now united with Peter Martyr, he occupied himself with establishing Protestant churches in Lucca, and other towns of Italy, the hatred of the Catholic priesthood increasing in proportion as his success was the greater, till at last, having undergone great persecutions, Ochino was banished from Italy. Being invited to visit England, he received a most hospitable reception from the Protector Somerset. After the accession of Mary to the throne, and the commencement of persecutions against the Protestants, he was obliged to quit England. He then wandered through Belgium, up the Rhine to Bâsle, where he remained for some time, occupied with the affairs of the Church, and preaching to the different congregations of Italian emigrants who had been obliged to leave their country, where persecutions were being carried on with such terrible severity.

---

NOTE. Page 40.—It must be admitted that Ochino, in his attempts to reform the manner of life of the clergy of Modena and Ferrara, and in the vigorous attacks he made on their depravity and luxurious mode of life, was well supported by the Court of Rome. On the 26th November, 1524, some years before the date of our narrative, Pope Clement VII., after effecting many reforms among the clergy of Rome, despatched a brief to the clergy of Modena and Ferrara, threatening them with excommunication and the loss of their benefices if they did not reform their manner of living, and cease wearing beards, velvet shoes, silk shirts, and other articles of dress inappropriate to their calling ; adding that the heretic Martin Luther, in the sermon he preached at Lamagna against the Papacy, brought forward the luxurious mode of life and dress of the Catholic clergy in proof of the errors of Romanism. In his brief his Holiness expressed his disapprobation in most emphatic terms, as the following extract from it will show :—

"*Debiano andare in habito da prete honesto, senza barbe, et altri portamenti dishonesti, come portano, de scarpe de veluti, camixe lavorate de seda, tagliate e con bragete deshoneste, et questi cussi vani erano certi zovenastri beneficiati, inamorati, li quali stariano bene in galea, e Martin Lutero alega questi portamenti in le so prediche che Lui fa in Lamagna contra al Papa, e S. S. ha fatto vestire la Corte da preto e più non vanno da sbrichi* (bricconi) *como facevano*" (Cron. Mod. di Tomaxin de Bianchi, nelle *Memorie di storia patria per le provincie modenesi*, vol. i. part ii., page 293).

# CHAPTER III.

## THE JUDGE.

AFTER Camille had left them, and the door had been firmly closed, the Judge received his friend with every demonstration of affection and respect. Finding Ochino almost fainting from fatigue, his first act was to set before him some refreshments, of which the ex-monk, exhausted though he was, but very sparingly partook ; for although he had some years before quitted the Capuchin order, and rejected as worthless many of their habits and customs, still he practised their abstemious manner of living. Setting apart the meat and wine which had been set before him, he contented himself with

some bread, fruit, and a glass of water.
During the simple repast, his host sat
opposite to him, silently watching him,
and it was not till he had concluded that
any continuous conversation ensued between them.   Ochino, having reverently
returned thanks to Heaven for the meal
of which he had partaken, his host said to
him—

"My dear friend, I hardly know whether
to be pleased or sorry to see you; for although the gratification of meeting an old
and dear brother in the faith is great indeed, I cannot disguise from myself the
terrible danger you have incurred in thus
visiting Ferrara."

"For years past," said Ochino, "I have
been so used to persecution and danger that
they have lost most of their terrors for me.
I have my work to perform, and the danger
must be more terrible than any I have ever
yet met which can deter me.   But first tell
me in what state is our holy cause at pre-

sent in Ferrara. Do those who have accepted the truth still hold manfully to it, or do the persecutions with which they are pressed drive them back to the errors of Rome?"

"Alas! my friend, here, as in every other part of Italy, the hand of the persecutor is strong upon us. Hundreds, under the pressure of punishment and intimidation, have succumbed. All right of public meeting for the celebration of our religion has been withdrawn, and even the act of meeting together for prayer has been adjudged criminal."

"But, surely," said Ochino, "that must be contrary to the laws of Ferrara? One of the principal boasts of your citizens was, that liberty of conscience was permitted throughout the whole Duchy of Ferrara. Has that law, then, been abrogated?"

"The law remains in our statute books as fresh as the day it was first made, and the Duke himself, on his accession to power, swore to maintain it. But while in the cases of the Jew, the Idolator, or the Mahometan, the law still remains in its full force, it is denied, under the most severe penalties, to us Protestants."

"But how can you, as a Judge, sworn to administer the laws without partiality, allow your Protestant brethren to be persecuted contrary to the spirit of the law you are called upon to administer?"

"I am helpless in the case," said the Judge. "A power—that of the Inquisition —has been established in Ferrara, which overrules all laws but its own; a power which claims to carry with it its own absolution, sanctifying, as a service acceptable to God, acts which set all God's laws at defiance."

"But still you remain in power. Can you not, therefore, insist upon the law being carried out in its integrity? or do your brother Judges oppose you?"

"My brother Judges, though the majority

of them are Romanists, to do them justice,
have endeavoured to maintain the law
granting liberty of conscience to the inhabitants of Ferrara. Nay more, they
made desperate efforts to maintain it in
spite of the Inquisition itself. At last a
case arose which gave a fair opportunity
for a trial of strength between the civil and
the ecclesiastical law as administered by
the Inquisitors, and the result of the
struggle was the triumph of the persecutor.
A certain Giorgio Siculo, of whose efforts
in the cause of truth you may have heard,
was cited to appear before the Inquisition
on a charge of heresy, and some of its
officers were sent to arrest him; but on
searching his house he could not be found,
and his wife and family either could not or
would not give any information as to where
he was concealed, notwithstanding their
being threatened with punishment should
it be found out that they had not spoken
the truth. Still Siculo was nowhere to be

4—2

found. His wife was put to the torture, but nothing could extort the secret from her, if she knew it. The Inquisitors were determined not to be baffled of their prey, and not only sent abroad fresh spies to discover him, but offered heavy rewards to those who would betray him. They were on the point of succeeding, when late one night Siculo called on me, and begged me to use the power of the civil law to protect him, asserting that he had in no way contravened the laws of Ferrara. Nay more, that he had not even infringed the ecclesiastical law, inasmuch as he had never yet attacked the Church of Rome, although he had preached against its abuses."

"I trust you granted his request," said Ochino.

"I did. I concealed him in my own house till I had an opportunity of meeting in consultation with the other Judges. They all agreed with me that Siculo's was a proper case to try whether the ecclesiastical laws administered by the Inquisition were superior to the civil laws of Ferrara. When I told them that Siculo was concealed in my house, my brother Judges advised that he should be placed for safety in one of the cells used for the detention of prisoners before their trial in the Palace of Justice. This was agreed to. On the day before Siculo's case was to be publicly argued in court, he surrendered himself into the hands of the officers of the civil justice, and notice was sent to the Inquisitors informing them of the fact. When they received the intelligence, they immediately demanded that the prisoner should be delivered up to them, and incarcerated in the dungeons of the Inquisition, which possibly you may be aware has been established in the monastery of the Corpus Domini. This, of course, was objected to by the Judges, and the inquiry into Siculo's case was ordered to take place the following morning, so as to let it be conducted with as little popular agitation as possible. The rumour, however, had spread abroad among the Protestant population that the inquiry was to take place, and long before daybreak many people began to collect before the Palace of Justice, ready to enter when the door should be opened. As day dawned, and objects became clearer, some of them thought they distinctly perceived something hanging to the iron bars of one of the upper windows of the Palace ; and as the light became stronger, the object began to assume the shape of a human being. Broad daylight came, and, to the horror of every one, the figure proved to be the dead body of Giorgio Siculo, who had been in the night hanged at the bars of the Palace window."

" But by whose order ?" said Ochino, utterly aghast.

" That the order came from the Inquisition there can be no doubt," replied the Judge, " but beyond that all is veiled in mystery. My brother Judges, Catholic as they are, were indignant at the act, and a rigid inquiry was instituted; but not a word could be heard, nor a fact learnt, which could throw the faintest light on the matter."

"But you surely do not mean to say that your investigations were attended with no result?"

"My friend, if you knew the state in which we now live in Ferrara, you would be but little surprised."

"How, then, is your public worship conducted?" inquired Ochino.

"Public worship, my friend," said the Judge, "has long since been abolished. As I told you before, the ecclesiastical courts have declared it penal. Nor can we worship together privately, for so completely is Ferrara deluged by spies, that if three met for private worship, the probability is that one of them would be a traitor. And how can it be otherwise, when they are taught that it is acceptable

to Heaven to play the traitor on those
nearest and dearest to them ?"

" But the Duchess Renée," said Ochino,
" surely she has not withdrawn her protection from the suffering Protestants in the
city ?"

" No, her willingness to shelter them is
as great as ever; but, alas! her ability has
been greatly curtailed.  In consequence
of what his Highness has been pleased to
call her heretical opinions, he has separated
from her, and assigned to her the Palace of
San Francesco, where she now holds her
court; but even there a system of the most
complete espionage is kept up.  Although
she is allowed to have her daughters Lucrezia
and Eleanora with her, it is solely under
the condition that the Jesuit Father Pelletario has the superintendence of their
education.  With the exception of my own
daughter, Teresa, who, since the death of
my wife has acted as lady-in-waiting on the
Duchess, and a few other officials attached

to her person, all around her are bigoted Catholics."

A silence of a few moments now occurred, which was broken by Bernardino Ochino saying—

"You greatly grieve me by what you tell me respecting the Duchess, as my mission to Ferrara was almost purposely to see her."

"That she will receive you with a cordial welcome is certain," said the Judge; "but whether you will be safe, even under her roof, is very doubtful, so great is the anger of Rome against you. Do you intend stopping any time in Ferrara?"

"Only a few days. An attempt has been made to form an Italian Church in Zurich for those of our countrymen who have fled from Italy for conscience sake, and I am intrusted with the charge of organizing it. One portion of my mission was to spread abroad among the faithful the knowledge of the existence of this Church, to which they might fly for refuge when driven from their own country; and the second was to ask the pecuniary assistance and patronage of the Duchess. The first part I have to a considerable extent accomplished. By adopting my present dress I have been enabled to visit the churches at Aosta, Como, Lucca, and other towns, and, thank God! hitherto I have succeeded, although my labours have not been unattended with danger. But tell me, do you think the Duchess will be able to assist me?"

"Certainly she does not want the will; as for the means, it is different. So continuous are the demands on her charity in the city, that I am afraid she will be able to afford you but little help. However, you had better see her to-morrow, and ask her for an asylum. It will be better for you to seek protection in her Palace, for I tell you candidly, you will not be in safety here. With the exception of my friend

Camille and my daughter Teresa, there is hardly a soul with whom I am intimate on whom I could rely; and be assured that even powerful as the protection of the Duchess may be, it will not be more than sufficient to shield you from the attacks of the Inquisitors as soon as they know you are in the city."

"How should they know I am here?" said Ochino. "I have told no one my name, and I entered the city at dark, by the gate of San Giorgio, purposely avoiding the Palace, and keeping my cowl well over my features along the whole road. Beyond an ignorant old man whom I found in the marshes, and your friend Camille, I have spoken to no one."

"Still you are not in safety; for although I can fully depend upon Camille, who knows but the old man was a spy sent to dog your footsteps, or that he has not already given notice of your arrival? A law has been established, ordering, under

the penalty of a heavy fine and a severe
flogging, that notice shall be given to the
police of any stranger entering the city, no
matter in how humble circumstances; and
of this you may be certain, that your arrival
is already known. What answer did you
make to the porter at the gate of San
Giorgio?"

"I did not speak to him," said Ochino.
"The old man my companion imagined
that, as I was in the dress of a Capuchin
Friar, I intended lodging at the convent;
and I did not undeceive him."

"And to-morrow the convent will be
visited, and as the superior will certainly not
be able to give a satisfactory answer to the
inquiries, spies will be set upon your track.
There is but one means by which you can
escape, and that is by obtaining the protection of the Duchess Renée. Although,
as I said before, her power is greatly
diminished, still her spirit and courage are
unabated; and if she offers you an asylum

in her Palace you will be safe, unless you
fall a victim to some hidden plot. True,
since the accession of his Majesty Henry II.
to the throne of France, the fear of offend-
ing a French princess is less in the eyes
of Rome than it used to be. Still the experiment would be a dangerous one, as her
Highness would be little inclined to allow
an insult of the kind to be offered her with
impunity."

"You stated that Pelletario, the Jesuit,
is now confessor to the daughters of the
Duchess. If I were to reside in the Palace
he would be sure to recognise me, for we
were formerly intimate."

"Of Pelletario you have less to fear than of
any of the others. He is a learned man and
an elegant scholar, and I do not think that,
unless stimulated by a very strong motive,
he would take any overt act against so
distinguished a man as yourself. No, all
things considered, you cannot do better
than appeal to the Duchess for protection.

To-morrow morning, early, I will send to my daughter Teresa, and tell her to inform the Duchess that you have arrived, and that you request an interview with her. At the same time, let me advise you to change your dress for that of a civilian. To appear at court in the one you now wear might expose you to danger—for being no longer a brother of the order, you have no right to it. But you must be tired with your day's journey. I will now show you to your bed-room, where you may remain in perfect safety at any rate till to-morrow, as, from motives of prudence, I allow no servants to sleep in my apartments, and therefore, beyond Camille, no one will know that you are here."

Ochino and his host now rose to separate for the night, but before doing so the former said, " But tell me who is the young man who conducted me into your presence ? From what he told me, he seemed to be an intimate friend of yours."

"His father is a merchant in Geneva, and an intimate friend of the illustrious John Calvin. When young, Camille entered the French army, but quitted it to study law, and became a pupil at the university. He was introduced to me by one of the professors, and has since been a constant visitor at my house. I almost look upon him as a pupil, for although I relinquished my position as professor at the university when I was appointed senior Judge, I still feel sufficient interest in him to continue the superintendence of his studies. Next year he is to return to Geneva, where he intends to commence practice. I will introduce you to him, and I am sure you will like him. You will doubtless be requested by the Duchess to preach in a small chapel she has fitted up in the Palace, the only place in Ferrara where a few can gather together to hear the Word. It will be indeed a pleasure to us all, for it is now some months since we have been able to join together in worship; for although her Highness, when we have a preacher bold enough to visit us, would willingly receive all those thirsting after the truth, the experiment is too dangerous to allow it to be often repeated. But I will detain you no longer, my friend. Sleep securely to-night; you shall not be disturbed. When breakfast has been prepared, I shall dismiss my servant, and you may then leave your room in safety. Afterwards I will conduct you to the Palace."

The Judge then showed Ochino his room, and the two friends separated for the night.

## CHAPTER IV.

### THE DUCHESS.

LTHOUGH the Duchess Renée no longer resided with the Duke in the Este Palace, it can hardly be said that a direct separation had taken place between them. He continued to treat her with marked respect and attention, and supported her in all matters except those connected with religion; and her authority seems to have been as much respected in Ferrara during the absence of her husband as that of the Duke himself.

For many years Renée appears to have wavered between Protestantism and Romanism, greatly favouring the former, while at the same time openly professing herself

a member of the Romish creed. Although
we find her sheltering Calvin, Ochino, Pietro
Martire Vermigli, Clement Marot, and many
other Protestant celebrities, and accepting
with pleasure the dedication of Bruccioli's
translation of the Bible into Italian, we find
her, outwardly at least, joining in several
Catholic ceremonies without hesitation.
Even as late as the year 1543, Muratori
tells us that the Duchess, attended by
seventy-two ladies, dressed in black silk
ornamented with gold embroidery, all on
horseback, followed by many carriages filled
with other ladies, and by the Duke himself
with a *cortège* of noblemen and gentlemen
on horseback, rode out to the gate of San
Giorgio to meet the sovereign Pontiff Paul
III., when he visited Ferrara. They then
accompanied him in his procession to the
Cathedral, where he celebrated the Pontifical
Mass, and presented the Duke with a golden
rose, and a sword and hat, which he had
blessed. The Duke testified the greatest

joy at the honour the Pope had done him,
and kissed the feet of his Holiness with the
utmost reverence. Renée's attendance at
this mass is emphatically recorded by more
than one of the Roman Catholic historians
of Ferrara, as proving that at that time her
Highness was still a faithful child of the
Church of Rome. Muratori also tells us
that the Pope, when he quitted the city,
presented the Duchess with a costly diamond, and a jewel composed of diamonds in
the form of a flower, in addition to many
gifts to her children.

Renée's attendance at mass on the occasion of the visit of Pope Paul III. was her
last, it appears, for many years; in fact from
that time her opinions seem to have taken a
decided change in favour of Protestantism,
till at length she openly renounced the
Roman Catholic faith. Of the proximate
cause of the change it would be difficult to
form any correct conclusion, though it is
more than probable it arose from disgust at

the duplicity shown by the Pontiff on his visit to Ferrara, and her abhorrence of the cruelties of the Inquisition which were afterwards practised by his authority, and which tribunal he had, when visiting Ferrara and expressing all outward love and affection for its inhabitants, brought with him in his train, and established in the city. Two years later his Holiness addressed a brief to the authorities of Ferrara, requiring them to institute a strict investigation into the conduct of every person, of whatever rank or order, suspected of entertaining erroneous religious opinions, and after having taken depositions to apply the torture, and when the trial was completed to transmit the whole process to Rome for judgment.

It was on the publication of this order of the Pope that Renée appears first to have openly opposed the Church of Rome, which she did by taking under her protection the Protestants of Ferrara, and that with so much vigour, that for five years the order of the Pope remained little better than a dead letter. But while the Duchess and her advisers, true to the policy of the Protestant Reformers, boldly denounced the errors of their antagonists, and sought by open argument to support their cause, the Inquisition adopted the usual crafty policy it was in the habit of showing when its opponents were strong. The Inquisitors established agents in all parts of the city, who set secretly to work, endeavouring by every means in their power to undermine the new principles which had taken root throughout the whole of Ferrara.

So vigorous was the onslaught made by the Inquisition, that resolute and courageous as the Duchess Renée had become in the Protestant cause, she seemed almost paralysed at the power brought against her; and for some short time appears considerably to have relaxed her wonted energy. In fact, so little opposition did she appear to offer, that those who had hitherto looked upon her as their champion, now seemed to lose heart. The news of her inaction at last reached the ears of Calvin, who was then resident in Geneva, and for whom she always appeared to entertain a great respect. In a letter written to her, and which is still in existence, he begs of her again to exert herself in the cause of the unfortunate, and to protect those suffering for religion's sake, urging her particularly not to listen to the arguments of the priests attached to her court, who would lead her from the truth.

She appears to have received fresh impulse from Calvin's letter, and her protection of the Protestants not only became more open, but she now boldly announced herself one of their number, and succeeded to a certain extent in stopping the violence of the persecution. At length a circumstance occurred—the death of Francis I. of France —which deprived her of a good and powerful ally. From Henry II., himself a bigot, she could expect no support, and the Inqui-

sitors knowing this but too well, carried on
their persecutions with greater vigour, and
even implored the Duke to incarcerate his
wife, unless she returned to the Catholic
faith.

The Duke, though willing to oblige the
Inquisitors, had too much respect for his wife
to obey their request, and he hesitated to
proceed with anything like severity against
the mother of his children and a daughter of
France. The inquisition still pressed upon
him the necessity of insisting on his wife
again adopting the Catholic faith, and the
Duke promised he would take the subject
into his serious consideration, although he
would not do so until he had tried every
conciliatory means of bringing her round to
what he considered a better frame of mind.
With this intent he commissioned his confessor, the Jesuit Pelletario, to argue with
her in order to convince her of the error of
her ways, and endeavour by every means in
his power to induce her to return to the

Church of Rome. The Duke's policy, however, was useless, for Renée would not listen
to the arguments of the Jesuit, and even refused to receive him into her presence, and
this was done in so open and abrupt a
manner as to rouse the anger of the Duke,
who determined, on his part, to show some
of that energy which his wife possessed in
so marked a degree. He now told her, with
an amount of determination which must
have surprised her, that for the future he
should no longer consider her as his wife,
but that to prevent open scandal he would
resign to her the Palace of San Francesco.
Here she could maintain a court of her own,
where her authority would be as strictly
obeyed as if she were residing with him in
the Este Palace; but her two daughters
were no longer to be with her.

This was indeed a cruel blow to Renée,
who was most tenderly attached to her
children; and she earnestly implored her
husband to alter his decision. Angry as

the Duke was at what he considered the obstinacy of his wife, he had still too much respect for her to be indifferent to her entreaties; while, on the other hand, he was strongly urged by the Inquisitors to maintain the resolution he had come to. At last a compromise was arrived at. Her two daughters were allowed to remain with her under the sole condition that she should not tamper with their religion, and that they should be under the spiritual care of the Jesuit Pelletario. All other members of her court, Renée was to choose for herself, and they were to be allowed, while under her roof, to practise the Reformed religion. The Duchess had no alternative but to accept these conditions. She removed to the Palace of San Francesco, choosing her officials as much as possible from Protestant families, though even among these there was too much reason to believe many were but spies in disguise.

As soon as Renée heard of the arrival of

Bernardino Ochino in Ferrara, she immediately offered him shelter and protection, at the same time advising him to assume some other name, for powerful as her protection still was within the walls of San Francesco, it would hardly be sufficient to defend him from the fury of the Inquisitors did they discover he had had the audacity again to make his appearance in the city.

In the afternoon of the same day, Ochino, in the quiet dress of a citizen of Ferrara, accompanied by the Judge Rosetti, proceeded to a secluded door of the Palace which opened into a back street, and which had already been used for the purpose of sheltering the fugitive and the oppressed.

On their arrival, the door was opened from the interior by an aged servant of foreign aspect, who conducted Ochino and the Judge up a narrow staircase which led into a corridor, from whence a door opened into a private room. Here they were ushered into the presence of the Duchess, who was attended by Teresa Rosetti, the daughter of the Judge, and another lady in waiting.

On seeing Ochino enter, the Duchess rose from her chair to receive him. When he bent on his knee to kiss her hand, she raised him, and insisted on his taking a seat by her side. After a few conventional sentences of welcome, the Duchess said to him—

"Have I correctly understood Teresa Rosetti that the object of your visit to Ferrara is to obtain help for the establishment of a church and refuge in Zurich, where those persecuted in Italy for the truth's sake may fly for shelter and protection?"

"It is, noble lady," said Ochino; "and I trust with your powerful assistance I shall be able to accomplish it."

"Alas! my friend," said Renée, "my power, as Rosetti will tell you, is but limited indeed." Then noticing an expression of doubt on Ochino's countenance, Renée continued—"Nay, believe me, I do not speak without experience: my power is almost gone. If you doubt me, inquire what was the fate of Fannio of Faenza. In vain did I use my authority to save him."

" And is it really true," said Ochino, "that the worthy man suffered for the faith? When in London, I heard that he had been arrested and put upon his trial; and although I knew how much he had raised the anger of the Court of Rome by his preaching, I thanked God that he had so powerful a protector as your Highness, and I felt assured that in the end he would escape."

"Alas! you far over-rated my powers," said the Duchess; "and yet to save him I exerted them to the utmost. He was tried by the Inquisition, and having openly avowed that he was a Lutheran, was judged guilty and his sentence sent for confirmation to Rome. A month afterwards he was burnt in the Piazza, and his ashes thrown into the river. Although discouraged by my failure, I still exerted myself to save

others, but all in vain. You may depend,
however, upon what little authority I have
being used in your favour. But were you
well advised to undertake this mission yourself? Had you written to me, I would
have been equally willing to aid you without your incurring the terrible risk you do
by visiting this unhappy city."

"I well calculated," replied Ochino, "all
the chances that would be brought against
me, although I admit I was little prepared to
hear how terribly our cause in Ferrara has
fallen. Still I fear nothing. The same
God who protected me in the different
cities I have traversed on my road hither
will protect me here. But should He in
his wisdom allow me to fall into the hands
of the persecutor, I am convinced it will
be for some good reason, and I shall submit to my fate with resignation."

"It shall be from no fault of mine," said
Renée, "if you do not quit Ferrara with
as much safety as you entered it. At the

same time, great prudence and caution must be used. You are too well known here not to be recognised if you are seen abroad, and therefore I would advise you not to leave the Palace. While within its walls, I trust I shall be able to protect you, though even of this I am not certain. Once seen outside your doom will be sealed. How long do you intend to remain among us?"

"The extent of my visit will not be beyond a few days," said Ochino, "as I wish to proceed to Venice, where I have some friends who will also protect me, and where I expect to receive liberal contributions to my work."

"Are you aware," said Renée, "that the Inquisition is also established in Venice, and that you will hardly be safer there than in Ferrara?"

"Pardon me, your Highness," said Ochino; "although the Inquisition is certainly established in Venice, the council would only allow it under the condition that a judge of the civil law should sit on all cases, and have equal power with the Inquisitor; and that unless both concur in a judgment, it should not be carried out. In Ferrara, on the other hand, as we have too good reason to know, the civil law is powerless against the Inquisition. In Venice, believe me, there is far less danger than here."

" Well, that being the case, thought must be taken in what manner you can reach Venice."

" Possibly the safest and easiest plan will be for me to descend the river till I reach Commacchio, where there will be no difficulty in finding a vessel to carry me to Venice. But before leaving Ferrara," continued Ochino, "I trust I shall have an opportunity of seeing and exhorting those of our faith to have courage under persecution and continue in the right way."

" It would be cruel indeed on my part," said Renée, " to attempt to deprive them of

so great a consolation, and every assistance
I can afford, both to them and to you, I will
willingly give. This evening after nightfall
(for it would be dangerous to attempt it
earlier) my private chapel shall be prepared,
and all those of our religion whom I can
trust, shall be invited to attend. Our congregation," the Duchess continued, smiling
sadly, " will appear small indeed compared
with that you addressed the last time you
preached in Ferrara, when, you remember,
our immense Cathedral was far too small to
hold those who rushed to hear you. But
be assured of this, a more devout assembly,
or one more earnestly seeking consolation
and encouragement, no preacher ever had,
than those who will meet here to-night.
Still they must be selected with care and
caution, for unhappily there are many of the
children of Judas among us, who would
readily betray their Master."

The conversation then turned on the Protestant cause in Switzerland, and especially

in Zurich. Afterwards Ochino narrated to the Duchess the different adventures he had passed through since he had escaped from Italy, dwelling particularly on his sojourn in England, and the friendly reception he had received from the Protector Somerset.* The intelligent, though somewhat plain features of the Duchess, kindled up with indignation when, with all his graphic powers, Ochino described the persecutions in Smithfield, and the cruelties practised on the unfortunate reformers after the accession of Mary to the throne.

"And is the monarch of that country a woman?" asked Renée. "I blush for our sex. O that I had been in her place!" She continued to pace the room backwards and forwards for some time, none caring to interrupt her in her exhibition of indignation, when suddenly she turned round to Ochino —" But how long has this monster been on

---

* See Note 1, page 92.

the throne? I thought the monarch of England was a young king." Then turning sharply on Teresa, she said," Was it not the catechism written especially for his instruction that I ordered to be translated into Italian, and printed in Venice?* How is it possible, with such a religion as that teaches, that the English people can have again relapsed into Romanism?"

"But your Highness," said Ochino, " his Majesty King Edward VI. died when quite a youth, two years since; and the Princess Mary, who had been educated in the Catholic faith, instigated by her husband, Philip of Spain, commenced a system of terror and persecution, to drive what they call heresy out of the land."

" Do you think they will succeed?" asked Renée.

" There is no chance of it, your Highness," replied Ochino. "The Queen and

---

* See Note 2, page 92.

her husband but little know the temper of the people over whom they rule. The great mass of their subjects are sincere Protestants, and although out of respect for the laws they may submit for a time to the persecutions, depend upon it, every fresh funeral pile which is lighted in Smithfield but hurries on the day of retribution."

" Is the Queen then not beloved by her subjects ?" inquired Renée.

" As little as it is possible for a monarch to be. Great as may be the love of the English in general for their monarchs, all seem to look with satisfaction rather than pity on the infirm state of her health."

" Is her malady considered fatal ?" asked Renée.

" So it is stated, your Highness ; but, of course, I am no authority on the subject."

" And who will be her successor ?"

" The Princess Elizabeth, it is believed."

" And what religion does she profess ?"

inquired Renée. " Is she still in the errors
of Romanism, or has she adopted the
reformed faith ?"

" A warmer supporter of the Protestant
faith does not exist in Europe," replied
Ochino. " The eyes of all Protestants are
turned towards her. Probably it is the
hope that she will soon succeed to the
throne, and that only, which keeps the
English people from rising against the
present Queen."

The conversation continued some time
longer on the same subject, and Renée then
gave orders to an attendant that an apartment should be provided in the Palace where
her visitor should not be subjected to inter-
ruption. The audience with the Duchess
then terminated, upon the understanding
that at nightfall they should re-assemble,
with as many Protestant friends as possible.

After the Duchess had left them, Rosetti
introduced his daughter to Ochino. There
was no little pride in her father's counte-

nance as he did so, for a more lovely young girl than Teresa it would have been difficult to find in Ferrara. She was about seventeen years of age, slim and graceful and of that peculiarly fair complexion which is so often found among girls who have been brought up in the neighbourhood of marshy lands, but without the sickly appearance which generally characterizes them. Her features were delicate—an exquisitely formed nose, a small mouth, large dark confiding eyes, black and finely traced eyebrows, an open clear forehead, and beautiful golden hair, which hung down her back and over her shoulders. In the expression of her countenance there was something extremely ingenuous and amiable, conveying an idea of truthfulness so strongly marked, that it appeared impossible, under any circumstances, to doubt a word she uttered.

Ochino was evidently struck with the beauty of the young girl, and expressed much pleasure at seeing her. He entered freely into conversation with her, and told her that he had two daughters, who with their mother were now in Bâsle, and that when times were more settled he hoped he should have the pleasure of introducing them to her. Then turning to Rosetti he said—

"If I remember rightly, you had another daughter; is she also living under the protection of the Duchess?"

"Alas! my friend, I have now but one child. My other daughter died with her mother during the last visitation of the plague in Ferrara. Teresa is the only relative left me in the world."

"It is fortunate," said Ochino, "to have found for her so powerful a protectress as the Duchess."

"I am happy to say her Highness is not the only protectress she has," replied the Judge. "Protestant as my daughter is, the two young Princesses have conceived for her a great affection, and she is allowed

to associate with them freely, under the
express stipulation that no conversation on
religious matters passes between them."

"Are you not afraid," asked Ochino,
"that, acting as they are under the authority of the Jesuit Pelletario, they may
endeavour to persuade her to quit the true
faith?"

"In the first place," said the Judge,
taking his daughter's hand, "I am sure my
dear child is too strongly imbued with the
principles of her faith, to dread anything,
either from the teachings of the Jesuit
Pelletario, or the influence of her young
friends, much as she is attached to them.
But there is still another safeguard for her.
When the Duchess took up her residence
here in the Palace of San Francesco, it was
expressly stipulated that if her Highness
did not attempt to interfere with the
religion of her daughters there should be
no interference with those of her court who
professed the Reformed doctrines, and I

am bound to say, at all events as regards my child, that no attempt has hitherto been made to tamper with her faith."

The conversation was here interrupted by a message from the Duchess requesting Teresa's presence. Bidding her father and Ochino farewell till they should meet again in the evening, she immediately left the room. As soon as she had quitted them Ochino said to his friend,—

" You must feel your house dreary indeed without the presence of your amiable child."

" That I would willingly have her with me is true," said her father ; " but after all it is a great consolation for me to know she is in a place of safety. Were she residing with me I should be under a double anxiety. First, from the continual attacks which would be made on her religion, and in the next place, from the admiration she would be likely to excite among the youths of Ferrara, for I cannot shut my eyes to the fact, and without a father's prejudice in her favour, that her personal attractions are of no common order. Were she to reside in my house under the care of a *gouvernante*, it would certainly be a great satisfaction to have her near me, but then again, her being in greater security under the same roof with the Duchess, relieves me from the anxiety I might otherwise feel. As it is she has the power of visiting me, accompanied by one of the elder female attendants of the Duchess, whenever she pleases, and on my part, I have free entrance to the Palace. But now, changing the conversation, are there any particular persons whom you wish invited to meet you this evening? If so, you have but to name them, and I will take means to request their presence."

Ochino now mentioned the names of several he wished to see.

" Alas! my friend," said the Judge, "not one of those you have mentioned are to be found in Ferrara. More than one has already suffered death for righteousness' sake, several are in the dungeons of the Inquisition, and others have fled for refuge to Switzerland. You will find no longer among us those bright names which shed so great a glory over Ferrara. Not one among them has been allowed to remain. Even the twenty-four ladies and courtiers professing the Reformed faith, who arrived with the Duchess in Ferrara, have all been banished, and those that now serve her are permitted to do so solely because it is imagined they are not possessed of sufficient intellectual faculties to be of the slightest danger to the religion of the State. Still, the faith is strong among us, although it is scattered, and we dare hardly whisper our religious belief to those who are nearest and dearest to us. Between this and nightfall, I will, assisted by Camille Gurdon, invite as many of our faith as may be safely trusted to meet us at the Palace, and when

our prayers are over they shall be severally
introduced to you. Although your visit to
Ferrara may have been attended with great
fatigue and danger, you will have the satisfaction of knowing, when you quit us, that
you have done good service in our cause, by
renewing in the bosoms of many of us some
hope for the future. I will also endeavour
to collect funds for your work in Zurich,
and I have every reason to hope my appeal
will be responded to with liberality. Many
ardent adherents of our creed are still to be
found among the poor and ignorant, but
among the educated and wealthy the proportion is still greater. Now 'excuse me,
my friend, if I leave you. I have no doubt
her Highness will see you again before
evening. You had better arrange with her
in what way you should leave Ferrara, for
although the longer you stay with us the
greater our satisfaction, the precautions
which must be taken to insure your escape
will occupy some time, and the sooner we

commence preparations the more likely they are to be carried out in safety."

NOTE 1. Page 81.—On his arrival in England Ochino seems to have received a very warm welcome, not only from the young king and the protector, but also from the principal Protestant theologians. Shortly after he had reached London he wrote a very curious and clever work, now almost forgotten, on the unjust pretensions of the Pope of Rome. Being then but little acquainted with the English language, he wrote it first in Latin, and then requested his friend Master John Ponet, D.D., to translate it for him. It is printed in black letter, and was published in the year 1549 :—

"To the Most Myghtie and most excellent Prince Edwarde the Syxthe, by the Grace of God, King of England, Fraunce, and Ireland, and on earth Supreme head of the Church of England and Ireland, Bernadinus Ochinus Senensis wisheth all Felicitie."

NOTE 2. Page 82—.This Catechism appears to have been translated into Italian by Florio, with the title " *Catechismo, cioe forma breve per amaestrare i fanciulla ; la quale di tutta la Christiana disciplina contiene la somma. Tradotta di Latino per* M. A. Florio." Small 8vo, but without place, date, or printer's name. The existence of this work was unknown to the learned Dr. M'Crie, yet it was inserted in the first Roman index, in the list of books strictly prohibited, and must therefore have been well known.

# CHAPTER V.

## " WHERE TWO OR THREE ARE GATHERED TOGETHER," ETC.

S predicted by Renée, the meeting in the evening to hear the preaching of Ochino formed a singular contrast to that which a few years before had taken place in the Cathedral. Then the body-guard of the Duke were called out to maintain order among those who rushed to hear the celebrated man; now, the few who wished to be present, quietly and stealthily made their way in the darkness of night, in the shadow of the projecting roofs of the houses to the back entrance of the Palace, carefully and timidly glancing round to see if they were watched, or followed, and frequently turning out of their way if they met any one whom they, rightly or wrongly, suspected. Singly, or at the most in groups of twos or threes, they arrived at the wicket door of the Palace, which was speedily opened to them when they knocked; and they were received by Camille and an aged female attendant of the Duchess, who conducted them to the private chapel, where seats were assigned them. As they took their places, and offered up the customary short prayer, before uncovering their faces they glanced stealthily round to ascertain whom they knew, looking suspiciously on the others lest there might be some traitor to the cause. By degrees, however, they became bolder, and smiles of congratulation, brotherly love, and welcome, became perceptible on their countenances, and low whisperings passed between them. And then again, as others entered, the eyes of those already assembled would turn on

them, eager to distinguish whether they
were friends or foes, and as they were recognised, a smile of greeting passed between
them, and so on with all fresh comers, till
at last the chapel was completely filled.
All suspicion then appeared to vanish, and
a look of unfeigned satisfaction, kindness,
and affection seemed to illumine the features
of the whole congregation. One thing was
particularly noticeable among the assembly.
Although many women were present, there
were no children or young girls, proving
that parental love had been too powerful to
allow them to expose their offspring to the
dangers which might attend a meeting of
the kind. It was nearly nine o'clock before all had arrived; and the Duchess
and ladies of her court then entered
and took their seats in front of the pulpit,
which was shortly afterwards occupied by
Ochino.

The service strongly resembled that in
use among the Congregationalists in En-

gland in the present day. Some hymns of great simplicity and beauty were sung, and different portions of Scripture, both in the Old and New Testament, were read in Italian from Bruccioli's translation.* A lengthened prayer of great fervour and piety was offered up by Ochino, and then, after another hymn had been sung by the congregation, he rose to commence his sermon. His text was Acts xvii. 23.

The first portion of his address consisted in drawing a comparison between the difficulties and dangers experienced by the Apostles in promulgating the doctrines of Christianity among the idolators, and those experienced by the Reformers of the Church of Rome in abolishing its idolatries and abuses. He then went into a lengthened description of the persecution the brethren were at that time suffering in all parts of Europe. He drew a vivid picture of what

* See Note, page 125.

the faithful were then enduring, extending
from England in the north to the extreme
shores of the Mediterranean in the south,
from the eastern extremity of civilized
Europe to the most western point of Spain.
He dwelt with great force on the cruelties
practised upon the unoffending Reformers in
the latter country, and showed how the
Inquisition, which had there taken even
firmer root than in Italy, tyrannized over
the souls and bodies of men, dissolving the
most sacred ties among them—the love of
the child for the parent, and the husband
for the wife. The priests taught that the
nearer the tie of relationship, the greater and
more pleasing was the sacrifice to God in those
who denounced to the Holy Tribunal the
Protestant tendencies of their relations. He
then passed over to France, where he described the noble efforts of the Reformers
and the persecutions which were brought
to bear on them. He informed his hearers
that when the temporal authorities seemed

disposed to show mercy, the priests had sent to Spain for Oriz the Inquisitor, a man to whom the sentiment of pity was unknown, to assume the direction of the Inquisition in that country. Thanks, however, to the spirit of justice in that noble nation, it was yet undecided whether he would be allowed to remain, as the persecutions he had organized disgusted even the most bigoted of the lay members of the Catholic Church in France. He showed them how the Catholic princes of Germany were striving, though ineffectually, to stamp out the Reformation; how in Flanders the Spanish governors, stimulated by the officials of the Spanish Inquisition, had already executed more than sixty thousand Protestants. Even in England, that country which displayed so glorious an example to the rest of Europe in setting boldly at defiance the despotism of the Church of Rome, a bigoted Catholic monarch sat on the throne, persecuting with relentless fury all who would not submit to the dominion of the Pope, and banishing from the hospitable shores of the country those sufferers for the truth's sake who had fled to it for protection in the previous reign.

"But, my friends," continued Ochino, "let us now turn to the brighter side of the picture. Notwithstanding the machinations of the Inquisition in France, and the imprisonments and executions suffered by the Reformers, the cause of truth appears to be daily gaining ground, and the courage of the persecuted rises. In Germany, with each fresh persecution, Protestantism seems to take stronger root. In the Netherlands the blood of martyrs so freely shed has had but the effect of creating more converts. In England, Heaven not only supports the persecuted, but the whole nation, indignant at the cruelties practised, will but for a very short time longer submit to them. The health of the present monarch is failing fast, and the Princess, her successor, is strongly attached to the Reformed doctrines. And although I cannot state that the prospects of our Church in Spain and in our own beloved country are at present very hopeful, depend upon it, the justice and power of the Almighty are too strong to allow the persecutor to continue his course unchecked.

"And now, my friends, I have come to the most painful part of my discourse. I have heard with deep sorrow that many of our dear brethren have again relapsed into the errors of Romanism, and practise the idolatry of the mass. Painful as their fall is to us, we should not sorrow as those without hope, but energetically try not only to shield and support to the utmost of our power those still among us, but endeavour to recall back again into the fold those who have quitted us. Remember that the Holy Scriptures prove to us, that those who have been weak in their faith have occasionally risen again into strength. They tell us that, although St. Peter in fear denied his

Master, his courage rose again, and like a true soldier of the Cross, he bore it to the death. At the same time, this episode in St. Peter's life is not given us as an example to follow, but one to avoid. It teaches us to understand the infinite mercy of Christ in again receiving into his love his weak-hearted disciple.

" But you may ask in what manner, while labouring under persecution, or in daily dread of some active oppression, and un-guided by the ministers of religion, are you to escape the snares which beset you on every side? Here, my dear brethren, let me point out to you the unappreciable advantage possessed by you over those who are members of the Church of Rome. Although the presence of a minister of religion is advantageous, you have that, in the absence of your minister, which may guide your footsteps with unfailing security—the Holy Scriptures, which are now circulated among you in your own language, so that all may read and understand. The whole College of Cardinals cannot more clearly enlighten a believer in the Church of Rome, than that book is able to enlighten the poorest among you. Let me beg of you, then, to study it attentively, and if you earnestly pray to the Lord to give you the gift of understanding, rely upon it your prayer will not be made in vain.

"Is it not a great consolation taught you in that Book, that you have the power, without the intermediation of the priesthood, to apply directly to the Almighty for protection and assistance? Explain, then, candidly your disease to the Great Physician, show Him openly your wound that He may heal you. Is it not the direct and special function of Christ to destroy sin and wash out all our iniquities? Never forget that God is all-powerful, and that without his permission not a hair can fall from your head. Do not allow yourselves to be influenced by following the example of the multitude, but only that of the saints. Let the word of the Lord be as a lamp before you, for if you do not read and believe the word which was written for your enlightenment, you will find many stumbling-blocks in your path through the world. The Lord knows that in addressing these exhortations to you, I am actuated only by the interest I feel in your spiritual welfare, and I trust you will receive my words as I mean them. I pray God to enlighten you and strengthen you in Jesus Christ, that you may triumph over Satan, the world, and the flesh, and in the end obtain the crown which belongs only to those who have conquered. Amen."

When Ochino had concluded his sermon, the breathless silence which had hitherto reigned in the chapel was partially broken, and a murmur of admiration arose. Another hymn was then sung, a short parting prayer offered up, and the service terminated.

But instead of the congregation quitting the chapel, they flocked round the pulpit, eager to approach nearer to the preacher when he left it, and that with so much earnestness, that it was difficult to keep them from inconveniencing the Duchess and her suite. When Ochino descended the pulpit steps, the Duchess advanced towards him, and warmly thanked him for his admirable discourse, carrying with it, as it did, consolation and comfort to the minds of those greatly needing them. The commendations of the Duchess finished, the congregation now threw off all subjection, and earnestly thanked the preacher for the encouragement and the consolation he had given them, which they assured him they would treasure up in their hearts to strengthen them in the days of persecution. So earnest were they in their manner of addressing him, that Ochino, accustomed as he was to the compliments and praise of those who heard him, was not proof against it, and the tears rolled down his venerable face as he thanked them for their kindness and good feeling. Possibly his tears might have been in some part caused by the idea which doubtless crossed his mind, that in a short time those who now pressed so eagerly around him, would be given over into the power of the persecutor, in whose hands no mercy would be shown them.

Among those who came forward to kiss the hand of the preacher was the venerable mother of the celebrated Olympia Morata, who had long since been obliged to fly from Ferrara to avoid the persecution with which she was threatened ; for neither youth, talent, beauty, nor all combined, seemed capable of exciting a spark of pity in the minds of the Inquisitors. When the old lady, now in her eightieth year, was introduced to Ochino, he received her with great respect and affection. He told her he had had the pleasure of seeing her daughter and her husband as he came through Heidelberg, and described the love in which they were held by the inhabitants of that city, and how much Olympia gloried in the fact, that in spite of all the persecutions which had taken place in Ferrara, her venerable mother had kept true to the faith. Then again were introduced to Ochino many of the relatives of those who had been banished, or had already suffered death for the truth's sake, to all of whom he had some kind word to say.

So cheering was the influence of that one man on the few members present of the Protestant flock which yet remained in Ferrara, that all seemed to forget the misery which surrounded them, and the dangers with which they were threatened. Instead of dispersing they formed themselves in knots, and entering the corridor leading to the chapel, conversed together with great friendliness. The Duchess Renée also greatly exerted herself to please her guests, conversing with them with

much affability.   Among the many to
whom she spoke, there was not one whom
she addressed with greater condescension
or kind feeling than Camille Gurdon.  She
complimented him warmly on the exertions
he had shown in the cause of truth, and
begged him still to go on in the same
way, and that he would receive his reward
for it in the next world, and not impro-
bably in this as well.

As she said this, Camille, involuntarily,
perhaps, cast an anxious glance on Teresa,
who stood by the side of the Duchess.
The glance, however, was unperceived by
Renée, otherwise she might have arrived
at the conclusion, that the hope of the
reward entertained by Camille Gurdon in
this world was not so far distant as she
herself imagined.   But if his behaviour
passed unnoticed by the Duchess, not so
by the young girl who stood by her side,
and a blush as deep as crimson spread over
her face, which seemed to have so painful

an effect on her that she dropped behind
the Duchess. Gurdon, also, perceiving the
effect his glance had produced, blushed
deeply and cast his eyes on the ground.
The Duchess noticed him, and mistaking
the cause of his confusion, said to him,

"Nay, do not feel embarrassed at what
I have said to you, but go on in the same
honourable course you have hitherto done,
protecting the unfortunate, administering
comfort to those in distress, and keeping
together in the fold those whom the wolves
among us would destroy. I have frequently heard of your good works, and
now, on my own part, and that of my
fellow-sufferers, I thank you for them."
Then turning to Ochino, who had now
joined them, she said, "A more useful or
energetic member of our congregation we
have not among us, and I only hope that
Heaven will grant him health and strength
to continue the good work he has put his
hand to."

Ochino also complimented the young man on the interest he had taken in the movement, and they then entered into conversation on the position and hopes of the Reformers in Geneva. Camille explained to him how strong was the influence of Calvin among the churches in that part of Switzerland, and with what devotion the inhabitants of the town regarded him.

"And may they long continue to do so," said Ochino, "for he is one of our brightest lights."

"Earnestly I wish," said Renée, "he would again visit us, although I am afraid there is but little chance of our seeing him. In a letter I received from him a few days ago, he told me, that much as he wished to visit Ferrara, so numerous and responsible were his calls, that it was, at any rate for the present, impossible for him to come here. Many were the messages he sent to different friends in the city, some, alas!" continued Renée, with much sympathy in her tone, "to those who within the last year have suffered persecution unto death for their adherence to the truth. He also inquired as to the progress of the school which he established for the poorer members of our community on his last visit here,* but which, I am sorry to say, has for more than two years been abandoned."

"To hear your Highness say so pains me greatly," said Ochino. "The continuance of his school would indeed have been a benefit, training up, as it did, in the right way, the children of those too poor or too ignorant to guide them themselves."

"Had we been allowed to continue the school without opposition, your remark would have been perfectly true," said Judge Rosetti, who had now joined the group. "We found that the children were tracked to their homes by spies, and thus many of those who belonged to us were detected by

---

* See Note, page 125.

the Inquisition. Emissaries were immediately sent to insist on the children being
sent to the Romish schools.   If the parents
obeyed, and they consented to attend the
mass themselves, by way of proving that
they had not joined the Protestant faith,
nothing more was said on the matter ; but
if not, the children were taken forcibly from
them, and the parents themselves im-
prisoned. With such power brought against
the poor and ignorant, you may easily
imagine that many relapses occurred ; and
sorely as it went against our consciences, or
rather against our wishes, we considered it
more prudent to close the school."

"But," said Renée, with considerable
pride in her tone and manner, " if we have
been obliged to close our school for children,
we have on the other hand established one
for adults, which is succeeding beyond our
expectation. Near the Palace of the Con-
sandolo we have a mission, which is making
converts, and although they are far from

being as numerous as those who leave us, still we have sufficient success to show that the wish to join us has still great strength."

"Are the Inquisitors aware of the existence of this mission?" inquired Ochino.

"Fortunately, up to the present time they have remained in utter ignorance of it," said Renée, "and I trust they may continue so till at any rate we shall have gathered sufficient strength not to dread their attacks."

"At the same time," put in the Judge, "I am in daily fear that it will come under the notice of the Inquisition. However, Providence has favoured us up to the present time, and that without our taking the slightest pains to conceal the movement."

While the Duchess conversed with great animation with the group which had gathered round her, a conversation scarcely less animated was carried on among the other guests, all touching on the difficulties and dangers which surrounded the Reformers in Ferrara. By degrees the conversation took a higher tone, and among the younger men the question began to be entertained, whether they would not be justified in the eye of the law in offering open resistance to the persecution they were suffering, some maintaining that the Inquisitors had far outstripped their powers in taking from the civil judges the jurisdiction of all ecclesiastical cases, involving the liberty and lives of the laity. In one group especially this question was argued with great vigour. Some advocated passive submission to the power of the Inquisitors till Heaven should, in its own good time, deliver them from the hand of the persecutor; whilst others maintained that the acts of the Inquisitors being illegal, all were justified in opposing them. At last one of the speakers turned round to Camille Gurdon, and asked him in what manner his countrymen would behave if treated with similar injustice.

"I have some diffidence in answering your question," replied Camille. "I am here a stranger receiving hospitality from the authorities of Ferrara, and I hardly know whether I should be justified in so doing, as it might be considered that I was putting before you a bad example. But although I may be somewhat outstepping the bounds of discretion, I will without hesitation admit that in my own beloved country, no matter whether Protestant or Catholic, not for one week would a state of things be allowed to exist such as at this moment reigns in Ferrara. From our first union as a nation to the present time, we have always resented any arbitrary or despotic interference with our laws, and we have ever felt sympathy with those suffering under persecution."

"In what manner, then, would you advise us to act?"

"There I can give you no decided answer," said Camille.

"But as a lawyer yourself you ought to be able to advise us."

"Nay, you do me too much honour in calling me a lawyer," said Gurdon. "Here I profess myself to be only a student. Why not put your question to one more competent to answer it?" he continued, seeing Rosetti advancing towards them. "Here comes your senior Judge, and one of the most learned lawyers in Italy. Why not ask him for his opinion?"

The eyes of the whole group now turned on the Judge, and they made room for him to join them as he, with Teresa leaning on his arm, approached.

"You all look at me as if you had some question to put to me," he said. "If so, let me know what it is."

"We were debating whether in point of law we should be justified in openly resisting the Inquisition, and we appealed to

8—2

Camille Gurdon for his opinion. He refuses, however, to give it us, fearing that
by so doing he might be considered guilty
of urging us to rebellion against the laws of
Ferrara, which he would not be justified in
doing, considering he is receiving hospitality from the State."

"Gurdon is quite right in declining to ·
answer a question of the kind," replied the
Judge; "for the interference of a foreigner
in the affairs of another country is always
looked upon with jealousy."

"But he referred us to you for an
opinion," said a law student who was
present.

"And I must decline giving it," said
Rosetti, "beyond stating that I hold the
present behaviour of the Inquisition to be
utterly illegal. At the same time, between
holding that opinion and advising you to
open resistance there is a wide difference.
Setting apart the question of legality, the
imprudence of an attempt at open opposi-

tion must be apparent.   Not only in
Ferrara might it bring down the power of
the persecutor more terribly upon us, but it
might stimulate to further action the power
of the Inquisition in other cities in Italy
where our Protestant brethren are less
numerous than they are here, and their
means of defence comparatively smaller. No ;
be assured the best power for us to look to
for help in this cause is Heaven, though, I
suppose," he continued, turning to Camille
Gurdon, on whose handsome face a flush of
honest indignation was plainly perceptible,
"you sturdy Republicans think differently,
and would rise against the oppressor, no
matter how great the odds might be."

" Candidly, Judge Rosetti, while respecting your prudence, I must admit it is
hardly the sort of argument we are accustomed to hear in my country.   There,
the greater the number of the persecutors
the greater and more energetic the resistance of the persecuted, their energies

and courage rising in proportion to the strength of the oppressor. Pardon me if I say it, but it would have pleased me more had I heard you adopt a different style of argument. You doubtless think me presumptuous in addressing with so much candour a man of your experience and learning; but trust me, it arises from no want of respect on my part, but is due to the education and example I have had continually before my eyes from childhood upwards."

The young man spoke with so much honest indignation that a murmur of admiration arose from the whole group, which had now considerably augmented in numbers, others being anxious to listen to the arguments carried on. Gurdon seemed to have inspired the younger portion of his audience with no inconsiderable share of his own animation; nor was the admiration confined solely to them. The ladies of the group seemed equally pleased with his address and manner, and none among them

more so than Teresa Rosetti, who gazed on
him with undisguised satisfaction.

" My dear young friend," said the Judge,
" believe me, no one present admires your
enthusiasm more than I do. But you must
remember that we have a different power
to contend with here from what you have
in Switzerland, and a system that will
answer with you would hardly succeed with
us."

" But why not first try the people before
coming to that conclusion ? Very possibly
you may find among them far more energy
than you calculate on."

" Camille," said the Judge, " you mis-
understand me. I have no fear of either
the courage or energy of my fellow-towns-
men. Still I hold that, demoralized as we
are at the present moment, it would be
impolitic to attempt physically to place the
civil law over the ecclesiastical. That in
your own country you can quote many
brilliant examples of independent thought

and action among the people is true, but
scarcely any more so than history records
of our citizens of Ferrara. Who sheltered
the fugitive Jews of Spain and Portugal
from their tormentors, and offered them an
asylum and protection more boldly and
resolutely than the citizens of Ferrara?
When in the time of Duke Ercole the
Great the Church claimed in Ferrara, as in
other cities, the right of sanctuary—that of
defending criminals who had rushed into
ecclesiastical buildings for protection and
shelter—did not we refuse to allow it, even
when the threat of the greater excommunication was brought against us? And
seeing our determined opposition, did not
the Pope himself give way? What people
ever fought more resolutely against an
oppressor than those of Ferrara under the
late Duke Alfonso against Pope Julius II.,
supported as he was by half Europe? Go
further back, and when the Inquisitor, even
with the protection of the Marquis Azzo

d'Este, stole in the night, from its tomb in the Cathedral, thirty years after his death, the body of Armanno Pungilupo, whom they had declared heretic, with the intention of burning it in the Piazza, did not the people of Ferrara attack the Inquisitor and the Marquis, and publicly replace the body in the Cathedral in spite of all the force which could be brought against them? No, my friend, believe me, native energy is no more wanting among the Ferrarese than among the noble-minded Swiss themselves."

The retirement of the Duchess to her private apartments was accepted as a warning by the assembled guests that it was time to leave the Palace. Nevertheless the leave-taking was so long that a considerable time elapsed before the corridor was clear. The happy evening they had spent, and the brotherly love their meeting had elicited, seemed to act like a charm which bound them together in a bond of unity it

was painful to break. At last the order of
their leaving was determined on, for short
as the passage might be from the
Palace to their dwellings, it was attended
with considerable danger. Some of the
younger, and among them Camille Gurdon,
proposed they should leave in a body, so
that they might be a mutual protection to
one another in case they should meet any
of the city guards on their road. The
graver members, however, objecting to any
display of force, suggested that they should
leave in small parties, so that if they met
any of the spies they might not excite
suspicion. This plan was at last adopted,
and the company slowly and gradually
began to disperse, till none were left but
Camille Gurdon and the Judge Rosetti.
They remained some time longer conversing
with Teresa and another lady-in-waiting,
with whose services the Duchess had dis-
pensed in order that Teresa might remain
some time longer in her father's society.

At last they also took their leave, Camille proposing to accompany the Judge to his home.

Rosetti and his young friend met with no impediment on their road. As they proceeded they conversed together almost in whispers, for fear of being overheard, on the events of the evening, especially on the preaching of Ochino. Camille appeared delighted with his eloquence. " I have heard," he said, " the best preachers in Geneva, including our great leader, John Calvin himself, but I never heard one who approached Ochino in eloquence. No wonder the court of Rome are so anxious for his apprehension. He is a host in himself, and were he again to preach in the Cathedral, and advocate the pure principles of the Reformation, he would convert all Ferrara."

" That he would do so if he could obtain the opportunity," said the Judge, " is most probable, but unfortunately such an experiment is not possible. Were it known that he is among us, he would immediately be arrested. Even during his lecture, and delighted as I was with it, I was unable to divest myself of the fear that among those listening to him might be some traitor that merely paid attention to his discourse for the purpose of denouncing him to-morrow."

"But surely," said Gurdon, "the Duchess would not allow him to be arrested in her Palace, and while under her protection."

"That she would oppose his arrest by every means in her power is certain," said Rosetti; "but I much fear in Ochino's case her power would be but of little avail. No, we must make what provision we can for his departure, and that as quickly as possible. Call on me early to-morrow morning, and let us talk over the matter."

Gurdon promised he would do so, and having now arrived at the apartments of the Judge, the two friends separated.

NOTE.   Page 96.—Although fragments of trans-
lations of the Holy Scriptures were to be found in
Italian libraries in the 15th century, the desire to read
them in the vernacular seemed to have spread in proportion (even among the liberal Roman Catholics themselves) with the march of Protestantism.  Rome, however, for some time strongly opposed the practice of
translating the Scriptures.  Even before the time of
Luther or Calvin, Papavanti declared that the Sacred
Scriptures were being degraded by being translated
into the vulgar tongue.  " *A virlire la sacra Scrittura
il tradurla in lingua volgare.*"   Some theologians went
so far as first to preach their sermons in Latin, and
then afterwards translate them for the benefit of their
congregation into Italian.   A Camaldolese monk,
Nicolo Malermi, translated the Scriptures into Italian.
His translation was printed in Venice in the year 1471.
It is said to have gone through as many as nine
editions in the 15th, and twelve editions in the 16th
century.   A proof, Dr. Thomas M'Crie says, that the
Italians were addicted to reading the Scriptures in
their native tongue, if there did not exist among them
at the time a general desire for the word of God.
Bruccioli's was the first entire edition of the Holy
Scriptures translated into Italian.   He dedicated it
by express permission to the Duchess Renée.   It is
said that as many as seventeen editions of it were published before its sale was prohibited by the Inquisition.

NOTE.  Page 110.—Although a strong tradition still

remains in Ferrara that Calvin during one of his visits to that city, organized a school to instruct children in the Protestant faith, and even taught in it himself, the statement must be received with great caution. True, a building near the spot where the Palace of San Francesco formerly stood is pointed out as Calvin's school, yet it is very doubtful whether such was the fact. The principal authority against it is the learned Luigi Cittadella, who is perhaps more deeply versed in the antiquities and history of Ferrara than any other modern writer.

## CHAPTER VI.

### TERESA'S VISITOR.

LTHOUGH it was still early when Camille Gurdon called on the Judge the next morning, he had already seen several of those who had attended Ochino's sermon the evening before. To the Judge's inquiries whether they had met with any impediments on their road home, Camille replied that they had met with none whatever, but that the streets had seemed singularly quiet and deserted. One or two had encountered the guard, but on replying when challenged, they were suffered to proceed unmolested. All seemed much pleased with their meeting, and augured that a greater amount of religious

freedom would be allowed them from the
fact, that so many could assemble and leave
without danger. So emboldened did they
feel, that several of them had requested
him to obtain permission from the Duchess
for another prayer-meeting to be held in
her Palace. Camille promised that he
would convey their wishes to the Judge
Rosetti, and implore him, should he see no
difficulty in the way, to apply to her Highness on the subject, as they considered he
had great influence with her.

"I will do so willingly," replied the
Judge, "although I am not certain it would
be unattended with danger. At the same
time a renewal of the peace and happiness
we enjoyed yesterday evening is too great a
temptation to be easily resisted. Still, if it
be done at all, we must lose no time about
it, as every day that Ochino remains in
Ferrara the greater his risk. Again, it is
impossible for me to wait on her Highness
this morning, as it is my turn of duty at

the Palace of Justice. But that difficulty may be overcome, I think. I will immediately write a letter to the Duchess, which I will get you to take, asking her again to grant the use of her chapel for our meeting, as it is the earnest wish of so many of her Protestant subjects in Ferrara. I will also say in the letter that the bearer, should her Highness require it, will give her further information on the matter."

A gleam of satisfaction was plainly visible on Camille's face when he heard the Judge's proposition.

" But I am afraid," he said, " I shall not be able to obtain an interview with the Duchess. She might consider it an act of presumption on my part were I to ask it."

" I did not propose that you should," replied the Judge, who was now seated at the table with the writing materials before him. " I intend merely to suggest that you would be able to give her the information should she require it. Nevertheless it would give me great satisfaction if you could contrive to obtain an interview with her. Possibly," he continued, "your better way would be to ask to see my daughter, and say that you have brought a message from me. Give Teresa the letter, and request her to place it in the hands of the Duchess. After she has read it, should she make any remark as to its contents, Teresa can inform her that you are waiting for a reply, and in all probability she will request to see you. I think you will have no difficulty in the matter. You are already well known to her, and I have mentioned your name in the letter. If you do see the Duchess, do not fail to impress upon her the danger Ochino is in, and the necessity there is for taking early steps to allow him to escape. That will arouse her to renewed energy, and she will come sooner to a determination as to the assistance she intends to afford him in establishing his mission church in Zurich. There is the letter, but before you go, tell me if you have thought of any plan by which Ochino may effect his escape to Venice."

"I have reflected but little on the subject," replied Camille, "but that little encourages me to think it may be done without much difficulty or danger, that is to say, provided few only are entrusted with the secret."

"The fewer the better," said Rosetti. "Have you then thought of a plan we could adopt?"

"I have," replied Camille, "and one in which it would be difficult to have fewer confidants. I propose hiring a boat, which shall be moored on the river bank a little below Mal-Albergo. As the current is at present strong and the river high, one other rower besides myself will be sufficient. I know a man who will suit my purpose admirably. He is a powerful, good-natured fellow, not over intelligent, and knows the river perfectly. I can easily frame some excuse to him and say I wish to row down the river a friend of mine, a Capuchin Friar (for Ochino must again wear his disguise), who is bound on a mission of mercy to some sick person near Commacchio. At daybreak when the city gates are opened, Ochino, with his cowl covering his face, and his wallet slung over his shoulder, can pass out, while I will be in waiting for him by the river-side, and once afloat, it will be difficult indeed to overtake us."

" Well, Camille," said Rosetti, " in your hands I leave the means for Ochino's escape from Ferrara. The plan you propose seems simple and feasible, and as far as I understand the matter, may be carried out with comparative security. At the same time, if you should consider it advisable to change it, or even make some alteration in it, let me know, and I will assist you as far as is in my power. You had better now no longer delay your visit to the Palace, and it is also nearly time for me to take my seat in Court. Meet me here this evening, and let me know what has been decided on."

On arriving at the Palace, Camille Gurdon had some little difficulty in getting his message taken to Teresa Rosetti. On his explaining that he came from the Judge her father, and that he had a letter from him to deliver, the porter asked him for it. Camille, declined, however, to give it to any one but Teresa, saying that, in asking for a personal interview with her, he was only carrying out the instructions of the Judge. A messenger was now sent to the private room of the young Princesses with whom Teresa then was. On receiving the message Teresa inquired who had brought the letter, and was told it was a young well-dressed Signore, who spoke with a slight foreign accent. Teresa, from the description, easily identified the messenger as Camille, and a slight blush suffused her face, which did not escape the notice of the Princesses, or of two elderly, discreet Catholic ladies, one of whom was a nun, who were present at the time. On noticing the effect the message had produced on Teresa, a significant momentary glance passed from the elder lady to the nun, while a good-humoured, malicious smile, almost amounting to a laugh, was indulged in by the young Princesses. Poor Teresa, finding that the eyes of her companions were fixed on her, hesitated what to do. The Princess Lucrezia, noticing her confusion, said to her—

"Nay, my dear Teresa, do not keep the foreign gentleman waiting."

"It was very kind of him to call at this dull Palace of ours on a message from your father," said the Princess Eleanora. "Pray, make him welcome, even if he is the arch-heretic Calvin himself."

"May I remind you," said the elderly lady, "that any conversation or allusion to matters of the kind are most distasteful to his Highness the Duke?"

"Oh! do not fear me, Donna Bonifazio. I do not intend to enter into any theological discussion. I have strictly obeyed his Highness on that point, have I not, Teresa, much as I love you? But once more, do not keep your foreign friend waiting; he will speak but lightly of our hospitality when he returns to Geneva if you do, for I suppose he comes from that city."

Teresa, perceiving that by going at once she would escape the jests of her friends, rose from her embroidery frame, and requested that Madonna Bonifazio would be present at her interview with the messenger, a request which was readily complied with. Leaving the room together, they passed through a corridor extending the whole length of the building, the apartments of the Princesses being at one extremity of the Palace, the private apartments of the Duchess in the centre, and the general public reception rooms at the other end. In one of these Teresa found Camille Gurdon. Being already fully convinced who her visitor really was, she advanced without hesitation to meet him, while Madonna Bonifazio, once in his presence, discreetly remained out of ear-shot. Camille explained to her the purport of the letter he had brought from her father, and his wish that if possible he should have an interview with the Duchess.

"Give me the letter," said Teresa, "and I will immediately convey it to the Duchess. I have no doubt whatever she will grant you the interview you desire."

Camille gave her the letter, and Teresa continued, turning to Madonna Bonifazio, "This gentleman has brought with him a letter for her Highness, and wishes for an interview with her. I will myself take her the letter and bring back the reply, and if you will kindly remain here in the meantime, I have no doubt I shall be able to return in a few moments."

Madonna Bonifazio now advanced and

entered into conversation with the young
Swiss on subjects of common interest,
taking care, although she believed him to
be a Protestant, not to touch on the for-
bidden subject of religion. The pair conversed together for some time, the lady
evidently pleased with the courteous manner
and language of the young foreigner. At
last they were interrupted by Teresa, who
returned with a message from the Duchess,
requesting to see Camille, and the three
then left the room together, Teresa and
Camille entering the apartments of the
Duchess, while Madonna Bonifazio continued onwards till she had reached those of
the Princesses. On her entrance they both
rose to meet her and eagerly asked for a
description of the gentleman who had called
to see Teresa. Madonna Bonifazio, however, seemed but little inclined to gratify
their curiosity, merely saying that he was
evidently a very courteous gentleman, whom
the Duchess, when she heard he had arrived,

requested to see. Nor, in spite of the rigid
cross-examination of the young ladies, could
they obtain anything more from her; and
the subject for the time dropped, though
evidently without the curiosity of the
Princesses being satisfied. They tacitly
resolved to question Teresa, when they
should see her. Shortly afterwards they
left the room to seek their own chambers,
and the nun rose from her seat to follow
them. The feminine weakness of curiosity
however, was as rife in the bosom of the
nun as in those of the young ladies,
although she had asked no questions in their
presence. Passing Madonna Bonifazio, she
said to her, in an undertone, " Who was
Teresa's visitor ?"

" I do not know more of him than this,"
was the reply—" if he is an emissary from
Calvin—he is evidently from Geneva—
and we are to have many such visitors, the
sooner Father Pelletario returns to the
Palace the better."

On being introduced to the Duchess, Camille Gurdon was received by her with great condescension.

"I have read your father's letter," she said to Teresa, "and I hardly know what reply to make him. He may be perfectly certain that my chapel is at the service of our brethren should they require it, but I much doubt whether it would be prudent to have another prayer-meeting so soon. Have you heard," she continued, turning to Camille Gurdon, "whether those who attended here yesterday evening received any annoyance on their road home?"

"I have seen several," was the reply, "and in no case did any of them receive the slightest molestation."

"I am most happy to hear it," said the Duchess. "However, I will speak to our Reverend Pastor Ochino, and ask his advice. All things considered, I think it would be better to delay another prayer-meeting, for a day or two."

"But pardon me, your Highness," said Camille, "I understood that his stay in Ferrara was to be very short."

"The longer he remains with us the better," said Renée, "so that he can do it in safety. While he keeps in the Palace there will be no danger of his being recognised, as none of the Catholic ladies of my court saw him when he was last in Ferrara."

"But is he not in danger of being recognised by the Father Pelletario?" remarked Camille. "Formerly, I understand, they were very intimate."

"The Father Pelletario is at present with the Duke my husband at Belriguardo," was Renée's reply, "and it is uncertain when he will return to the city. You have not heard the subject spoken of, Teresa, have you?"

"I heard Madonna Bonifazio say the other day that she had received a message from the Father Pelletario, stating that most probably he should remain at Belriguardo till the Duke's return to the city, and that they would arrive together."

"I do not expect his Highness will return before the end of the week," said Renée, "therefore we need be in no hurry for a day or two. I will talk the matter of the next prayer-meeting over with our Pastor, and let you know his reply. But now," she continued, addressing herself to Camille, "did I rightly understand you were a native of Geneva?"

"I am, your Highness."

"Are you acquainted with our great leader John Calvin?"

"I have spoken to him but once or twice," said Gurdon, "though I know many of his intimate associates, and have heard him preach frequently."

"Are you acquainted with any one residing in the same house with him?"

"Yes, more than one."

"Might I trust you, then," said Renée, "to convey to him a letter from me? I

received one from that good man a few
days since, in which he complains that I do
not write to him, and he trusts I am not
getting lukewarm in the faith. Now I
have written to him several times lately,
and he evidently has not received my
letters. Might I trust in you?"

"You may, your Highness," said Camille,
"as implicitly as in yourself. Confide to
me your letter, and my death alone shall
prevent his receiving it."

"Call on me this evening, then," said
Renée, "and the letter shall be ready for
you. If you succeed in transmitting it to
him, you will do me a great favour. But
now tell me, has any plan been suggested
for our Reverend Pastor Ochino to leave
Ferrara in safety?"

"I have conceived a plan by which I
think he may do so without difficulty or
danger," said Camille, "and one in which I
have not to fear the indiscretion or
treachery of any one;" and he then nar-

rated to the Duchess the plan he proposed adopting, on which he was much complimented by her Highness.

The interview continued but a short time longer, when the Duchess permitted Camille Gurdon to depart, requesting him to call in the evening for the letter she wished to forward to the great Reformer in Geneva. On leaving the room Teresa conducted Camille, as far as the ante-chamber. Before quitting her, he said—

"Do you think I shall have any difficulty this evening in being admitted into the presence of the Duchess?"

"None whatever," said Teresa. "You may rest assured every facility will be shown you."

"Still," said Camille, "I should hardly like to be conducted to her Highness by any one in whom I could not positively confide. The commission she has given me is a somewhat difficult one, and the fewer entrusted with the secret the better.

Would you object to be present at the time? You have already heard her mention her wish, and it would be advisable that no one else should know it. Now do oblige me."

"If you wish it I will be present," said Teresa, slightly colouring. "But now I must leave you to attend on the Duchess, so good-bye till evening."

Teresa then left him, and returned to the room she had just quitted.

# CHAPTER VII.

## A DANGEROUS COMMISSION.

N the afternoon of the same day, after the duties of Judge Rosetti at the Palace of Justice were over, Camille Gurdon related to him the interview he had had in the morning with Renée, saying how she was unable at the moment to give any decided answer as to allowing another prayer-meeting to be held in the chapel till she had spoken to Ochino on the subject. He further informed Rosetti that the Jesuit Father was then absent, and not expected to arrive in Ferrara till the Duke himself returned, and that no other person in the Palace would be able to recognise him.

"So far that is fortunate," said the Judge, "and it relieves my mind from a considerable amount of anxiety. Her Highness did not state when she would be able to give an answer respecting the prayer-meeting?"

"She did not," said Gurdon, "but requested me to call on her again this evening, when very possibly I shall have her reply. Her Highness also spoke on another subject," he continued, alluding to Renée's letter to Calvin, "which doubtless she would have no objection to speak of to you; but, as I have not yet received her authority, you will pardon me if I do not mention it. I have no doubt this evening she will authorize me to confide it to you."

"You are quite right, Camille," said the Judge, "not to divulge her secret till you have her authority for doing so. But I trust you will be on the alert as to any rumours respecting Ochino's presence in

Ferrara, and have the boat in readiness, that he may be able, in case of danger, to depart at an hour's notice.

Although the apartments of the Princesses were separate from those occupied by the Duchess, the most perfect freedom of access existed between them. Renée, as before stated, was tenderly attached to her daughters, and the love they bore their mother was that of devoted and affectionate children. Yet a singular feature existed in their family love. Tenderly attached as they were, and happy in each other's society, that great bond of family love — unity of religious opinions — was utterly wanting. It was their custom to meet together in the apartments of the Duchess each afternoon. Religion was then to them all a proscribed subject, under penalty of the absolute separation of the mother from her daughters; so that while the warmest display of family love was developed in their meetings, each had to

10—2

put a guard on her tongue lest the subject held most dear by her—religion—might come to her lips. And this must have been the more painful to them, as the Princesses were as ardently Roman Catholic as their mother was Protestant. At these meetings, on other subjects, the most unrestrained freedom of conversation prevailed. The somewhat taciturn habits of Renée would then relax, and she would enter, with the most perfect effusion of heart, into the details of her daughters' conversation,—into descriptions of their amusements, and consultations on dress—a subject which Renée, Frenchwoman as she was, generally appeared to hold but in slight estimation—and join in the innocent gossiping of her children with an eagerness which formed a singular contrast to her ordinary staid and somewhat reserved manner. In these afternoon re-unions the gaiety of heart developed in Renée and her daughters seemed also to communicate itself to the attendants, and Madonna Boni-

fazio, who accompanied the Princesses (neither
Sister Laura, the nun, nor Father Pelletario,
the Jesuit confessor, being ever admitted
into Renée's presence), and Donna Ponte,
an elderly Protestant Swiss from one of
the Italian cantons, would then converse together with the Duchess and her
children with perfect friendship and good-
feeling.

On the afternoon in question, a slight
difference was observed in the manner in
which the conversation was carried on.
The Duchess, intead of as usual occupying
herself with her daughters, conversed principally with the two elderly ladies. This
was probably due to the conduct of the two
Princesses, who had tried to draw Teresa
into a corner of the room, overwhelming
her with questions, half serious, half jesting,
on the handsome foreigner who had called
in the morning. All these Teresa, possibly
not displeased at the insinuations of her
companions that the real object of the

young foreigner's visit was herself and not their mother, parried as she best could; nor did she escape from her tormentors till a short time before the meeting broke up, when the Duchess called her daughters to her, and after conversing with them for some time on ordinary topics, dismissed them and retired to her own room, taking Teresa with her.

" I do not feel very well this evening," she said to Teresa; " my head aches, and my eyes smart. I have probably over-fatigued them by writing this long letter. I am not sure whether I shall be well enough to give an audience to your father's friend when he calls this evening, but I fear not. In that case, you had better see him yourself, Teresa. If you do, pray impress upon him the necessity of using great caution, so that the letter may not miscarry."

" If your Highness orders it, of course it is not for me to disobey," said Teresa,

" but at the same time——" and here she stopped short, as if afraid to conclude the sentence.

" I think I understand you, Teresa," said Renée. " You doubt the propriety of your seeing him alone, and I compliment you on it. But I had no intention of proposing it to you. You can have one of the ladies-in-waiting with you, so that no misconstruction can be placed on your interview."

" But in that case," said Teresa, " your secret would be confided to another."

" Hardly so," said the Duchess. " Take with you Donna Ponte ; you can speak French fluently, and she does not understand a word of the language. Converse then in French, and she will be ignorant of the object of your interview."

" Should she inquire," said Teresa, " what answer shall I make her ?"

" Refer her to me, that is all you have to do. Now, do not fail to impress upon

the youth the absolute necessity there is
that he should conduct himself with great
discretion in the matter, and that as much
for his own safety—or more so perhaps—
than mine; as, should he be discovered,
but little mercy would await him at the
hands of the Inquisitor.

"There is no occasion for me to dwell on
the last reason," said Teresa, somewhat
warmly. "My father's friend, Camille
Gurdon, requires no better stimulus for
energy and secrecy than the wish to obey
your Highness, and the success of our
cause."

"Well," said Renée, smiling at the
earnestness of the girl's manner, "if I
have done him an injustice I regret it.
Since, then, I have so devoted a servant,
tell him I rely implicitly on his discretion;
that I feel persuaded he will carry out his
commission with tact and energy. Tell
him if he succeeds I will give him a reward that shall prove to him my gratitude

for the service he has done me. Now take the letter, Teresa, and meet him when he comes, for I feel I shall not be able to see him myself."

Teresa took the letter and retired to her own room; and when there, attempted to think over, with a cool brain, the events of the day, and especially her conversation with the Duchess and her daughters in the afternoon. Although her conversation with the Princesses was in reality carried on more in jest than earnest, it had left a somewhat deeper impression on the mind of the young girl than she herself perhaps would willingly have allowed. Again, it must be admitted that she had already conceived a considerable amount of admiration for the handsome and talented young Swiss. But although she had met him often, little conversation had ever passed between them, either her father or some female friend having invariably been present. Teresa's regard for the young fellow, however, had already reached that

point when simple admiration is about to
ripen into a warmer feeling, which her conversation with the Princesses that afternoon
had tended considerably to develop. Again,
there was another point which caused her
much consideration. What could be the
reward which the Duchess intended to present to Camille should he succeed in the
commission he had undertaken? There was
a mystery about it she could not unravel.
Could she have meant by it that Camille
Gurdon——

Before the thought had been perfectly
formed Teresa had already regretted it, and
felt angry with herself for having begun to
entertain it. But in spite of her reasoning
she could not divest herself of the impression that the Duchess had uttered the words
with peculiar significance in her tone and
manner. Then again Teresa rejected the
idea, and then again it recurred to her, and
thus alternately doubting and resolving the
time passed till evening had closed in ; and

then she began to collect her wits for the interview with Camille, postponing for future consideration the question whether the Duchess intended to present the young Swiss with her hand in case he should successfully carry out the commission intrusted to him.

Teresa now went to the apartments of Donna Ponte, to request her presence at the interview with Camille Gurdon. For some time Donna Ponte objected, as she did not consider it prudent on the part of Teresa to hold an interview with so young a man, and it was only after Teresa had shown her the letter of the Duchess (taking good care not to let her see the superscription), and assuring her that it was by desire of the Duchess she was to meet Camille, and that her Highness had wished her (Donna Ponte) to be present, that she consented, and they descended together into the large hall, where members of the household were accustomed to meet strangers who called on them. On their way thither a servant met them, who informed them that the foreign gentleman who had called in the morning had arrived, and wished to be presented to the Duchess; but as her Highness was indisposed that evening, he had come for instructions on the subject. He received for answer that the stranger was to be shown into the hall, and shortly afterwards Teresa and her companion entered, and found Camille awaiting them. Teresa immediately advanced to meet him.

"Her Highness," she said in French, "has requested me to see you, as it is not convenient at present for her to receive you. She told me to give you this letter, and impress on you the necessity of using great caution in forwarding it to its destination. I suppose I may inform her that you will willingly do so?"

"Most willingly," said Camille. "Tell her she may rest positively certain it shall be forwarded. And is there no commission I can execute for you?"

"None," said Teresa, somewhat surprised at the question, "beyond carrying out faithfully the wishes of her Highness."

"As I said before, that shall faithfully be done. It would increase the pleasure, however, if I had a commission also to execute for you."

"I have none," said Teresa, with something like agitation in her voice, "except requesting you to give my love to my dear father."

Camille remained silent for a few moments, and then said to her in a still lower tone of voice,—

"Oh! how I wish I could have but a few moments' conversation with you alone!"

"For what purpose?" said Teresa, assuming an air of surprise.

"I cannot tell you," he said, looking towards Donna Ponte, who, finding they were speaking French, had retired with something of ill-humour to some distance, so far, in fact, that she could scarcely be seen, for although the hall was lighted up by a brazen lamp in the centre, its rays were hardly sufficient to illumine so large a space effectually  Teresa was silent for a moment, and then said, with considerable hesitation in her voice,—

"You can speak if you wish.  My companion understands no French."

"Even if that were the case," replied Camille, "I have hardly the courage to address you on the subject I wish.  It is on the admiration I have for you, which began from the first moment I saw you, and which has gone on increasing since. In pity's sake tell me what I am to do."

"I can listen to no conversation of the kind," said Teresa, "without first receiving permission from my father and her Highness."

"Will you allow me, then, to speak to

your father?" said Camille, breathless with anxiety.

"I have no right to forbid you," said Teresa, puzzled what answer to make : "you can if you please." And then assuming more courage, she continued, "But I cannot allow you to speak more with me now, nor will I have any further conversation with you on the subject until you have spoken to my father."

"Answer me but one question," said Camille, "and I will obey you. May I tell your father you gave me permission to speak to him?"

"No, certainly not," said Teresa; "you must take it on your own responsibility."

"May I hope," asked Camille, "that you wish me success in my interview with your father?"

"I will not say another word on the subject," said Teresa, "and if you will not go, I must leave you, and that will appear uncourteous."

"I must obey you, then," said Camille, sighing. And then taking her hand and kissing it respectfully, he left the room.

As soon as he had quitted them, Donna Ponte said in a tone of ill-humour to Teresa, "I hardly think it was particularly civil to me, or proper bearing in a young girl, to converse with that stranger in French, knowing, as you did, that I do not understand the language. In my time young girls behaved very differently. Not a word ever passed between one and a young man without some staid elderly lady being present at the time."

"I told you," said Teresa, "that it was the express wish of the Duchess that you should be present at this interview, nor would I have received the stranger unless you had been there. What you say about my incivility in speaking French arose from no fault of mine. I had the direct instructions of her Highness on the matter."

Donna Ponte made a gesture of doubt of

so marked a description, that Teresa could not fail to notice it.

"I told you the truth," she said angrily, "and to morrow, in the presence of the Duchess, I will get her to confirm what I say. At the same time, I don't like to be treated with incivility or doubt by you. That you are my senior, I admit, but not my superior."

Teresa, finding that Donna Ponte was on the pointof making an angry reply, left her, and walked rapidly to her own room, nor did she leave it again that evening.

# CHAPTER VIII.

### ORIZ.

ON the morning after the Duchess Renée had despatched her letter to Calvin, a stranger in the dress of a Dominican monk, attended by two servants and three baggage mules, arrived at the convent of the Corpus Domini, and requested to see the Superior, Father Fabrizio. The lay-brother who received the stranger informed him that the Reverend Father was at that time much occupied in his private room, and had given orders that no one should disturb him.

"He will make an exception in my case," said the Dominican. "Pray take my message to him, and then see that my servants and mules are properly accommodated."

The lay-brother for a moment hesitated what to do, as the instructions he had received from his Superior were imperative, and Father Fabrizio, who at that time acted as the chief Inquisitor in Ferrara, was not a man likely to allow his orders to be broken with impunity. Still there was a calm self-possession in the stranger which puzzled the lay-brother very much. Although he spoke in a calm and almost subdued tone, he seemed to possess great determination of purpose, and his manner, though quiet and courteous, was still of a description which showed he not only was accustomed to command, but to be obeyed.

" Might I ask your name, Reverend Father?" said the lay-brother. " I fear unless I take it to Father Fabrizio there is but little chance of his seeing you, but far greater probability of my displeasing him."

" There will be no occasion to tell him my name," said the monk; " he has been expecting me for some time. Say to him that I only arrived this morning from Paris."

The lay-brother then left the room, and shortly afterwards returned with the Superior of the convent, who received the stranger with every mark of profound respect. He then invited him to accompany him to a private room which had been prepared for him, much to the surprise of the lay brother, who looked upon the Superior of his convent with great reverence, and he was naturally somewhat puzzled to know who the individual could be who was received with so much respect, justly concluding that he must be a man of the highest importance. Nor was he mistaken in his conclusion. The stranger was none other than the celebrated Oriz, than whom, though his title was no higher than that of a Doctor in theology, few of the College of Cardinals possessed greater power. This man had been appointed by Henry II. of France, his "Inquisitor of the Faith."

When first he commenced his duties he exercised them for some time with considerable
moderation. Tradition says of him, that he
was then of a rather jovial good-natured disposition. If true, all traces of it were completely lost at the time of our narrative.
It is even recorded of him* that in the year
1534, when he was sent as Inquisitor to
Sancerre to search for heretics, the inhabitants, aware of his fondness for good cheer,
treated him with so much hospitality, that
although Protestantism had really taken
great hold in the neighbourhood, he repor-
ted them to the *Lieutenant Criminel* as a
very good sort of people. He was then
as Dr. M'Crie says, but young, and had
not yet tasted blood.† Afterwards, spurred
on by the Court of Rome, he carried on
his labours with so much rigour, that he
became at last one of the most cruel per-

---

* Beze, " Hist. des Eglises Ref. de France."
† " Reformation in Italy."

secutors of the Protestants that ever disgraced the Romish Church in France. To such an extent did he carry his spirit of persecution, that although named by his Majesty Henry II. as Grand Inquisitor of France, the French papists were disgusted at his conduct, and insisted on his quitting the kingdom. For some time the King refused to listen to his people, but at last finding the discontent at the presence of the Inquisitor becoming prevalent in all classes of society, his Majesty determined to send Oriz on a mission to Ferrara for the double purpose of bringing the Duchess Renée back to the Romish faith, and by his superior energy and inflexible cruelty, to exterminate heresy in the strongest hold it had hitherto obtained in Italy.

As soon as they were alone, the Superior, in the same tone of marked respect which he had shown on first meeting the stranger, said—

" I hardly expected you so soon, Reverend

Father. You must excuse me if I was not prepared to receive you."

"Make no apologies," said Oriz. "I have arrived two days earlier than I taught you to expect, from the letter I forwarded to you; but understanding that my presence was much needed in Ferrara, I have made greater haste than I otherwise should have done."

"That your presence is much needed in Ferrara is perfectly true. It gives me also much pleasure to be able to resign the direction of our Holy Office into hands far more experienced than my own. But before we touch on that subject," the Superior continued, "allow me to order some refreshment, as you must doubtless be fatigued with your journey."

"Not at all," said Oriz. "I reached Mal-Albergo yesterday evening, where I remained for the night, and crossed the river this morning. The letter I received from you in Milan, tells me that for some time past little progress has been made in Ferrara in exterminating the pestilential heresy which afflicts it: is that the case?"

"It is," said the Superior. "And yet this has arisen from no want of zeal on my part or the part of those connected with me."

"From what cause does it arise then?" inquired Oriz.

"From the power her Highness still exercises over the Duke. Again, you must not imagine the inaction which has lately been observed has been without other cause. Having received the intelligence of your expected arrival, I thought it better to let things remain in abeyance till I met you, contenting myself with seeing that heresy made no head. My principal reason for this inaction was, that as her Highness is still indisposed to attend mass, and exerts herself for the protection of the heretics, I allowed her to carry out her designs with comparative impunity a little longer, judging that by the time of your arrival we should be better able to point out to you those who are the principal supporters of the errors of Calvinism in our city, and thus place in your hands information which it would have been difficult to obtain had we carried on our efforts with the same unflinching severity we did some months since."

"And have you succeeded?"

"I may say we have, and to an extent we had hardly calculated on. We have discovered, and in fact intercepted, many letters written from her Highness to the archheretic Calvin, and thereby we have become acquainted with many names of individuals tainted with heresy which we should not otherwise have known."

"Have you placed these intercepted letters before his Highness?" inquired Oriz.

"I have not," said the Superior. "I thought it better to await your arrival; the more so as I will candidly admit that the

Duke, although a true son of the Church in all spiritual matters, and of a fidelity not to be suspected, receives with considerable coolness, if not anger, any complaints of the conduct of the Duchess. You, with your superior authority, will, I trust, be able to remove that impediment. But I have some most pleasing intelligence to give you. The renegade Capuchin, Bernardino Ochino, is at this moment in Ferrara."

"Has he been arrested?" asked Oriz.

"He has not."

"And why not?"

"Because," said the Superior, "he is residing in the Palace of San Francesco, under the protection of the Duchess; but we have him there as securely as if he were at this moment locked up and in chains in one of our own dungeons. Our agents watch the Palace night and day. Not an individual can enter or leave it without our knowledge, although no one residing in the Palace or those entering it imagine they are watched. So complete is the system adopted, that it would be impossible for even a child to leave it without our being informed."

"Have you the names of those who attended the prayer-meeting there the other evening?" said Oriz.

"I have," said the Superior, evidently much surprised that Oriz was aware of the prayer-meeting having taken place. Possibly Oriz noticed the expression of surprise on the countenance of the Superior, but he made no remark.

"And you are certain you may depend upon the fidelity of those of your agents employed within the Palace?"

"I am as certain of their fidelity as I am of my own, and all, of any ability, have been removed from the suite of the Duchess. Those who now remain with her are principally aged women, whose intellects are none of the brightest, with the exception of a young girl, the daughter of Biagio Rosetti, the senior Judge, who is also tainted with heresy, and who, like her father, might be convicted of the crime to-morrow should proceedings be taken out against her. We have even gone so far as to obtain the removal of the tutor of the young Princesses the celebrated Francesco Porta da Creta, from merely the suspicion that he had imbibed heretical notions, and have obtained the appointment for the Jesuit, Father Pelletario."

"Why is that young girl allowed to remain?" asked Oriz.

"Partly because we did not wish to have the appearance of none but aged or infirm women being in attendance on the Duchess, who, I may mention, has resolutely refused to allow any one who attends mass, or the confessional, to be about her person, and partly because the two Princesses have conceived a strong affection for the girl. I trust you see no objection to the arrangement?"

"None whatever," said Oriz. "If the two Princesses are well instructed in their religious duties, as I have no doubt they are, there will be little danger to their souls, while we may hope—in time at least —that their double interest may act on the mind of the heretic girl. But now tell me if the Duke and Father Pelletario have returned to Ferrara?"

"Not that I know of," said the Superior; " but I hardly think it probable."

"So far to the contrary," said Oriz, "that it is more than probable they are at this moment arrived. When I reached Mal-Albergo yesterday evening, and found that the Duke was at Belriguardo, my first care was immediately to despatch a messenger to him, humbly requesting that he would grant me an interview, and that on the receipt of his answer I should make preparations to wait on him without delay."

"I should think then," said the Superior, " that his Highness will await your arrival at Belriguardo."

"I hardly agree with you," said Oriz,

coolly. "I think it more probable that his Highness will have left Belriguardo this morning to join me in Ferrara, and the distance is not so far but that he may have already arrived. You will greatly oblige me by sending a messenger to the Este Palace to know whether it is the case."

The Superior now left the room and despatched a messenger to the Castle, to inquire if the Duke had arrived from Belriguardo, but before he had returned with an answer, an officer of the Duke reached the convent with a message that his Highness impatiently awaited in the Este Palace an interview with the Reverend Father Oriz.

Oriz, with the alacrity which usually distinguished him in all matters he had undertaken, delayed not a moment, but returned with the messenger. On entering the audience room in the Este Palace, he found the Duke in conversation with the Father Pelletario, who had also returned to Ferrara with him. The reception which

Duke Ercole gave to the Inquisitor was one
of mingled friendship and respect, which
Oriz on his part received in his usual quiet
and subdued manner, without the slightest
appearance of gratitude or pleasure at the
welcome the Duke had given him. The
only semblance of marked expression on his
countenance was when the Duke introduced
him to the Father Pelletario. Then for a
moment he cast on the Jesuit a glance so
piercing, that he seemed as if determined
to read the confessor's inmost thoughts.
The glance Pelletario cast on Oriz was
scarcely less characteristic. While bowing
with profound respect and humility, and
with a smile of pleasure at the introduction,
the keen eye of the Jesuit fell on that of
the Inquisitor, telling him that he was as
perfectly able to defend himself as the Inquisitor to attack, and that he feared nothing whatever from his presence.

" You told me in your letter, which I received late last night," said the Duke, "that

you were the bearer of a mission of great importance from the King of France. Let me ask you whether it is one of such secrecy that the Reverend Father Pelletario cannot be present at our interview ?"

"It would give me great joy could I have the Reverend Father's advice and support for the subject I am about to introduce to your Highness. At the same time, as my message is to you alone, I hardly know whether I should be justified in the respect I owe to his Majesty, in allowing a third person, without his permission, to be present at our interview. I am, however, fully persuaded that had his Majesty been aware that that person would have been the father confessor to your Highness, he would not have made the slightest objection."

The Jesuit Father, on hearing the answer Oriz made to the Duke, immediately acquiesced in the propriety of there being no third person present at the interview, and, bowing respectfully to the Duke and the Inquisitor, left the apartment.

As soon as they were alone, Oriz said, " I sincerely trust your Highness will pardon me for having undertaken the painful mission with which I have been intrusted. I beg to assure your Highness I would willingly have avoided it, but his Majesty the King insisted so strenuously on my undertaking it, that I had no alternative. First, then, let me place in your hands an autograph letter his Majesty has sent you, and which you will find will corroborate all I say to you."

The Duke opened the letter, and glanced rapidly over it.

" I see," said the Duke, addressing Oriz, " that in this letter his Majesty tells me that at his earnest desire you have taken this journey to Ferrara, to speak to me on spiritual things concerning our state, and especially regarding our illustrious Duchess, the Princess Renée. I will presently read the letter again, and in the meantime will you give me your message?"

"Allow me, your Highness," said Oriz, drawing a paper from his pocket, "to refer you to this document, which has been drawn up by the express order of his Majesty. In it I am requested to implore your Highness with the utmost earnestness to allow me an interview with the illustrious Princess, the Duchess Renée, in the hope that I may be able to extricate her from the labyrinth of those unhappy opinions in which she is lost, so contrary and repugnant to our holy faith and religion, and the news of which has caused deep sorrow to his Majesty the King of France. At this interview I am also instructed to impress upon her the great favours God has granted her, and amongst others, that of being the issue of the present blood of the most Christian house of France, where no monster has ever existed; and also to explain that, should she remain in her stubbornness and pertinacity, it would displease the King as much as anything in the world, and would cause him entirely to forget the love he, as her nephew, bears her, he hating nothing with a greater hate than all those of the reprobate sects, whose mortal enemy he is."

"That you will have my full permission for the interview with the Duchess you may be perfectly assured, but at the same time, Dr. Matteo Oriz, you must not hold me answerable if she refuse to receive you. Excellent as a wife, admirable as a mother and in all other respects, her Highness is inflexible on any subject connected with her religion; and I profoundly regret to say that the hatred the most Christian King bears the reprobated sects he speaks of, is not greater than that in which her Highness holds many of the most eminent men of our holy religion, especially those who are members of the monastic orders. Should her Highness, therefore, object to receive you, do not consider me in any way guilty in the matter."

"It would be gross presumption on the part of so humble an individual as myself to judge your Highness in this matter," said Dr. Oriz; "nor should I venture to ask you to allow me to make a remark on it were I not commanded to do so by his Majesty, who takes the greatest interest in the soul of his dear aunt the Duchess Renée."

"Make any remarks you please; I will willingly hear them," said the Duke.

"His Majesty goes on to say," continued Dr. Oriz, glancing at the King's instructions open in his hand, "that if after such remonstrance and persuasion as I shall be able to make to her, so that she may know the truth, and the difference there is between light and darkness, she still remains unconverted, stronger means should be employed."

"I do not understand you," said the

Duke, with something of surprise in his tone not unmingled with severity.

"I am instructed by his Majesty," said Oriz, disregarding the Duke's tone of displeasure, "that in case I should be unable by the gentle means I shall use to gain her, and reclaim the Duchess, I am——. But pardon me if I here read my instructions verbally, that your Highness may not think I exceed them." Then reading, he continued—"'He shall take counsel with the said Lord Duke as to what can possibly be done in the way of rigour and severity to bring her to reason.'"

"The language is somewhat of the strongest," said Ercole, sternly; "and I am rather surprised to find that the King of France should write in such a manner respecting an illustrious Princess of his own house."

"His Majesty goes still further," said Dr. Oriz, continuing in the same respectful impassive tone; "he says that in case rigour or severity fail to bring her to reason, then his Majesty wills and approves, and indeed exhorts your Highness very earnestly, that you would cause the Princess Renée to be put into a place secluded from society and conversation, taking away her children and the whole of her family and court, entirely irrespective of whatever nation they may be. But," continued Oriz, "the instructions of his Majesty to me go still further with respect to the punishment to be inflicted on the noble lady should she continue in the error of her ways. As, however, the subject seems painful to your Highness, I will not allude further to it than to say, that his Majesty trusts your Highness will punish with unflinching severity, even to the death, all those who shall have assisted or abetted her Highness, as well as take all possible means of clearing from your dominions the heretics which at present infest them."

For some moments the Duke remained silent and thoughtful, as if undecided what answer he would give to the chief Inquisitor. Ercole had a difficult task before him. He was conscientiously grieved at what he considered the erroneous religious opinions entertained by the Duchess. For political reasons he was most anxious to continue in good favour with the Court of France. But above all it was his chief interest at that moment to keep on good terms with the Court of Rome, in order to secure the succession of the Duchy to his own children, instead of allowing it to revert — as it probably would after the death of his successor—into the States of the Church. Still, the naturally proud feelings of a Prince of the house of Este revolted at the idea of any foreign powers, even those as influential as the King of France, or the Pope of Rome, interfering with the domestic affairs of his principality. And this feeling was further increased by the natural sentiment of manhood which prompted him to stand forward and defend his wife from the powerful conspiracy which he could easily perceive had been formed against her, much as he objected to the principles of the religion she had adopted. The Inquisitor, who stood motionless, with his eyes fixed on the ground, perfectly understood the agitation at that moment swaying the mind of the Duke, but rightly judging that in the end his Highness would agree to the request of the King of France, he said nothing.

"Dr. Matteo Oriz," said the Duke, suddenly, "I submit to the demands of his Majesty the King of France, and you have my full permission to request an interview with the Duchess. With respect to the stronger portions of your instructions we will talk over them more hereafter. At present my permission is limited solely to an interview with the Duchess, although I think you will have some difficulty in obtaining it."

"If your Highness would advise the Duchess that a messenger has arrived from her nephew the King of France, who desires to speak with her, and that it is your especial wish the interview should be granted, I am fully persuaded she will then no longer hesitate."

"Probably you may be right," said the Duke, after a moment's consideration. "I will do so; but remember, Reverend Father, should you be displeased with your interview, no disrespect shall be shown the Duchess, nor shall any steps be taken against her or any person of her household without my especial authority."

"Your Highness may be fully persuaded I will carry out your orders," said Oriz.

## CHAPTER IX.

### AN AUDIENCE.

N the afternoon of the same day Oriz proceeded to the Palace of San Francesco, and had his audience with the Duchess. When he arrived at the Palace he was conducted to her private room in which she was accustomed to hold her confidential audiences. When he entered he found her Highness attended by two ladies, one of whom was Donna Ponte, already alluded to, and the other Teresa Rosetti. Till the Inquisitor was ushered into the presence, Renée had no idea that the messenger for whom her husband had demanded an interview was a monk. A slight flush of displeasure crossed her face when she saw him, but the moment after she controlled it. On advancing gravely to within a few yards of the chair on which the Duchess was seated, Oriz waited for her to address him.

"His Highness, the Duke has this morning sent me a message," said Renée, "that you have arrived from the Court of my nephew the King of France, and that you were intrusted with a special message for me. Did I correctly understand him?"

"You did, your Highness," said Oriz. "I am intrusted with a message from your Royal nephew; but as it concerns yourself alone, might I respectfully submit that no others should be present?"

"Before I answer you," said Renée, "tell me whether your mission treats on political, family, or spiritual subjects, for from your dress I suspect it must be the latter."

"Your Highness has arrived at a right conclusion," said the monk. "My mission, beyond some strong sentences of affection on the part of your Royal nephew, relates only to the welfare of your soul."

"Then, sir," said Renée sternly, "know that, as I have long since rejected both the mass and the confession, I now refuse to grant you, a monk, a private interview on any subject of the kind. These ladies have my fullest confidence, and you may, if you please, speak with the most unreserved candour. On any spiritual matter I have nothing to hide from them."

"I much regret the decision your Highness has come to," said Oriz. "May I hope you will reconsider it?"

"Certainly not, sir," said Renée. "Proceed with your message or quit the room. I will not be dictated to by any one, priest or noble."

"I will obey your Highness," said Oriz. "At the same time pardon me if I say that you place me in a very painful position. It would be painful to me under any circum-

stances, but in the presence of others it will
be doubly so."

"Proceed, sir," said Renée, somewhat
impatiently.

"My message from his Majesty, then,"
said Oriz, "is shortly as follows : that he
has heard with profound sorrow that you
have refused to attend the mass, and ab-
stained from the confessional — that you
have set at nought the different rites and
ceremonies of our Church, such as eating
meat on prohibited days, and setting bad
examples to those around you, besides other
grave faults. He sincerely hopes that you
will kindly listen to the arguments I shall
bring forward to show you that you are in
error."

"Proceed with them, sir," said Renée.

"Your Highness must perceive that it
will be inconvenient at the present moment
to attack the errors into which you have
fallen ; and to prove their falseness at a
single interview would be difficult to me

and fatiguing to your Highness. I trust that on another occasion you will allow me to go systematically into the subject."

"Why not proceed with them at once?" said Renée. "At any rate make your beginning."

"Still I must crave the indulgence of your Highness to grant me another opportunity."

"And if I refuse!" said Renée.

"My instructions with your Highness go no further," said Oriz. "All the rest relates to the Duke himself."

"And might I ask you," said Renée, "what those instructions are, or are they to be kept a secret from me, his wife?"

"Unfortunately," said Oriz, "they are not to be kept a secret from your Highness. On the contrary, they are to be most explicitly told to you. At the same time, I would prefer the Duke, your husband, explaining them to you."

"The Duke, my husband, explain them

to me!" said Renée angrily, grasping the arm of her chair. "And why can you not explain them to me yourself? Do not stand on any punctilio. I have received offence from those wearing your habit so often, that I am now able to bear any fresh one with composure. Say, sir, what it is you mean, for I perceive it is already on the tip of your tongue."

" If I must obey your Highness," said Oriz, " my instructions go to the extent of requesting the Duke to place such restraint on you as shall preclude the possibility of your doing injury to the souls of others ; and not to grant you your liberty again till you have consented to attend the mass and the confessional."

"In other words, sir, I suppose I am to be deprived of the society of those around me. You Inquisitors—for I can easily perceive you are one—appear determined to leave standing no opponent whom you can overthrow. One would have imagined

the bodyguard I have, two of whom you
see standing by my chair,"—pointing to
Donna Ponte and Teresa—"were not of
such a dangerous kind as to excite your
apprehension. But tell me, suppose that
even then I refused to hear you, what
would be the result?"

"Pardon me, your Highness, if I do not
answer that question."

"Nay, speak, man; why hesitate? Tell
the whole truth. I repeat again, if I refuse
to attend the mass and the confessional,
what then?"

"Once more I trust your Highness will
excuse me," said Oriz.

"What, ashamed of your mission?" said
Renée, sarcastically, "and you an Inquisitor!"

"I am not ashamed of my mission," said
Oriz, now drawing himself up, and showing
for the first time during their interview
that his countenance was capable of another
than the placid, resigned look it had

hitherto worn. "I am not ashamed of my mission; I glory in it. Know then the advice of his Majesty the King of France to the illustrious Duke your husband is, that should you continue still in your errors and impenitent, to apply those means for your conversion which have succeeded so well with thousands of others."

"And what may they be?" said Renée.

"The torture," replied Oriz emphatically.

"The torture!" said Renée, rising from her seat, with an intense expression of indignation on her countenance. "The torture! And that word applied to me, a Princess of France!" Then, advancing towards Oriz, she said, "It is false; my nephew never intrusted you with such a commission; he dare not do it. The whole manhood of the French nation would rise up with indignation were it known that he suggested a thing of the kind. And you would advise my husband, the Duke, to apply the torture to me, his wife? Do you

think for one moment that he would entertain the suggestion, attached though he
is to the Church of Rome? Have not
those of your creed already had good proof
of the temper of the Princes of the House
of Este when unjust interference was attempted to be used in the affairs of their
dominions? Ah! that I wore a beard, and
that you were not a priest," said Renée,
"licensed to insult a woman without danger. I would then show you what would
be the result of offering Renée of France an
insult of the kind. Try the experiment on
my husband, the Duke, if you please. But
no, though you would insult his wife, you
would not have the courage to propose it to
him."

"Not only have I the courage to propose
it to him," said Oriz, who had now completely resumed his ordinary tranquil tone,
"but I hold it to be an especial portion of
my duty, not only to your nephew, but to
that great cause whose humble instrument

I am, to impress its necessity on the Duke; and that the torture be repeated till your Highness has attended mass, confessed, and done penance for your offences."

For some moments Renée continued to gaze on the monk with intense indignation. Her anger, however, seemed not to have the slightest effect on Oriz, who stood before her cold and impassive as a statue.

"Once more, before I leave," he said to her, "let me implore your Highness to consent to listen to my arguments; for it will pain me greatly to inform the Duke, your husband, of your disobedience to his wishes."

Renée looked calmly at him for a moment, and then said—

"Not only do I refuse to hear you, but I insist that our interview now cease, and that you never seek to enter into my presence again; for, no matter on whose part you come, I will not receive you. Of what service can any argument on your part be, when the opinions of both of us are irrevocably fixed on articles of faith as wide as the poles asunder? You hold that the mass is a sacrifice appointed by God for the redemption and salvation of the living and dead. I hold such a doctrine to be an unbearable blasphemy, in which the passion of Jesus Christ is quite overthrown and set aside, as if it were of no effect whatever. I hold that our Blessed Saviour, in offering Himself up, presented Himself an eternal sacrifice by which our iniquities have been purged and cleansed, and ourselves received into the grace of the Father, and made partakers of the heavenly inheritance. I know you will tell me that you make the same sacrifice which Jesus has made, but I hold such an argument to be blasphemous, for that sacrifice can be made by no one else. You cannot fail to see that one of two things must take place: either I must acknowledge as true what I at present consider the horrible mummery of the mass, or,

if I admit your arguments, I must trample
under foot the cross of Christ. But the
crowning desecration which I should com-
mit would be the idolatry I should perpe-
trate by adoring a creature instead of God,
which is a thing I hold to be altogether in-
excusable, while you hold that it is all
essential to salvation. Our opinions being
so widely different, it would be useless to
argue further on them. You are not likely
to change yours, and certainly there is not
the remotest probability of my changing
mine."

"Pardon me, your Highness, if I submit
that the arguments you have used are not
yours," said Oriz, "and the opinions which
at present misguide you are not the result
of your own reflections. You have accepted
them from that arch heretic, John Calvin—
a man who, not content with reviling our
holy mysteries, and causing schism in
our Church by argument and open means,
attempts even to detract by personal slander

from the character of those good and holy
men who would help you in the right way.
Excuse me, your Highness," he continued,
seeing the indignation rise in Renée's face,
"but please to recall to your memory a
certain letter that John Calvin wrote to you
when he first began to tamper with your
faith.    Before commencing his arguments,
he tries to neutralise the confidence you had
in your chaplain by speaking of him in the
most disrespectful manner, and advising you
not to give credence to his utterances."

Astonishment for a moment took the place
of indignation on Renée's countenance; for
it was quite true that in one of the first
letters Calvin had sent to her on the mass,
he had strenuously advised her to give no
ear to the doctrines preached by her chaplain.

"I know not, sir, how you became possessed of the knowledge that I received such
a letter; but at the same time I admit that
that good and pious man did write me a

letter requesting me to beware of the doctrines and teachings of my then chaplain,
and grateful, indeed, was I to him for the
caution; for I afterwards discovered that
his knowledge of the man was correct. Have
I, then, such spies about me," she continued,
her indignation again getting the better of
her astonishment, "that even my private
letters are brought under the notice of the
Inquisition? That your duplicity was great
and skilful, I knew; but I hardly considered
it was carried to such a point. But our interview must now terminate. Use what
influence you please with the Duke, my
husband. Persuade him, if you can, to allow
the torture to be applied to me"—Renée
here stopped short for a moment, indignation
impeding the current of her words; but she
continued at last, "the torture for me, Renée
of France!"

"Yes, madam," said Oriz, quietly, "if all
other means fail. If prayers, entreaties, and
arguments are of no avail, better a thousand

to one that your body should suffer than that your soul should perish eternally. Nay, do not think," he continued, noticing the violent indignation which agitated Renée, "that it would be any indignity in such a cause to offer the torture to a princess of the house of France. High as your dignity may be, it has already been used, and with good effect, to princesses fully your equal. The Queen Juana of Spain has already suffered the torture of the cord, and with the happiest results. Her Majesty, who had for years refused to attend the mass and confess, after her punishment, to the great joy of her son, his Majesty Charles V., and the edification of all true believers, no longer offered any objection, but became a willing child of the Church. And doubtless your Highness, if we are pushed to that terrible necessity, will follow her example."

"You do not know me," said Renée, "if you think that any torture or any punishment you can inflict on me would make me desert those opinions which I have conscientiously adopted. Once more, I believe the celebration of the mass to be nothing better than execrable idolatry. I will part with my life itself sooner than admit the contrary. If you are honest you will take that answer to the Duke, my husband. Ponte," she continued, turning to her lady-in-waiting, "and Teresa, my child, bear witness to my determination. No power on earth shall induce me again to become a member of the Church of Rome! Now, sir, leave me; and, remember, I shall give orders to my servants never to admit you again into my presence."

Oriz, without changing a feature of his countenance, which remained perfectly calm and impenetrable, bowed respectfully to her Highness, and the audience terminated.

## CHAPTER X.

### AN ALARM.

ALTHOUGH the indignation raised in Renée's breast by the audacity of Oriz's language had supported her during their interview, it vanished shortly after he had quitted the room. For some time after he had left her she remained seated on her chair of state, which had been placed on a slightly elevated daïs, her features wearing a stern, dignified expression, as if she could hardly realise the fact that the Arch-inquisitor was no longer standing before her with calm determination stamped on his face. By degrees Renée's rigidity of feature began to soften, and she slowly turned her face to Madonna Ponte (who had stood on one side of her, and Teresa on the other) as if to seek for consolation and support; but she found none. The worthy Italian Swiss had been so shocked at the behaviour of the Inquisitor, that she had not yet been able to recover her self-possession, and she returned the gaze of the Duchess with one of mingled bewilderment and alarm. Renée then mechanically turned toward Teresa, and found that the tears were rapidly chasing each other down the poor girl's face. The sight of Teresa's tears had the effect of calling forth those of the Duchess. All the majesty of demeanour which she had hitherto maintained, and which, on occasion, she could assume with great effect,—although ordinarily she was simple and unpretending in the extreme,— now vanished, and, covering her face with her hands, and bending forward in the chair, she burst into an uncontrollable fit of weeping.

Astonished at the violent outburst of

grief of the Duchess, both Madonna Ponte and Teresa attempted to console her, though with little good effect. Donna Ponte, who had now fully regained her self-possession, endeavoured to show Renée the necessity for calming her feelings, so that with her habitual wisdom she might be able to guide, as well as protect, those who without her aid would be but as sheep led to the slaughter.

"Do not talk to me in that tone, Ponte," said Renée, at last, "for in my present misery it seems almost like mockery. What power have I?" she continued, raising her head and looking almost angrily at Madonna Ponte. "What support can I give to any when I am myself weak and powerless as a bruised reed?"

"Still," said Teresa, "your Highness has wisdom, and wisdom is power. Think how helpless the faithful in Ferrara will be without your aid and advice."

"My child, once more, what power have

I to help them?" said Renée, emphatically. "My wisdom! Look at me now," she continued, turning her face, covered with tears, towards the young girl; "look at me, and then say whether, crushed as my poor brain is by the heavy sorrow which oppresses it, I have the wisdom to guide others."

"Pardon me if I remind your Highness," said Teresa, "that there is a Power perfectly able to give you wisdom, and to point out the way to guide others with a certainty that all the princes of this world would in vain attempt to overthrow or oppose."

"True, my child. To that Power let us all humbly confide ourselves, and pray to be released out of the hands of the persecutor. But, should it not appear right in the eyes of the Almighty to place extraordinary power in my hands, of what use can I be in this matter? I am a woman, and at this moment as weak as either of you—

possibly more so. All the ability I once possessed was derived from others, who then supported and guided me. And where are they now? My illustrious relative and friend, King Francis, is dead, and my nephew, the present King of France, not only deserts me, but has sent the Inquisitor Oriz to persecute me and my Protestant subjects. The Duke, my husband, not only permits him to address me, but even to threaten me with imprisonment and the rack if I do not personally turn a traitress to my God, or if I attempt to shelter or protect any of the scattered sheep of Christ's fold in this city, who are now without a shepherd."

" But if your Highness has no longer the sword of the mighty to protect you in your present difficulty, you have still your wisdom left to guide you, which, with aid from the Almighty, may yet be sufficient."

" My wisdom, Teresa, is on a par with my power," said the Duchess. " I never possessed much, and, as I said before, the little I once had sorrow hath stamped out of me."

"Your Highness has already guided us in many difficulties and dangers, and may do so again," said Madonna Ponte.

"Never again, Ponte," said the Duchess. "What you are pleased to call my wisdom was really the wisdom of others, who had me for their mouthpiece. And where are they now who inspired me with that wisdom? All those learned men in my suite, who were my countrymen and Protestants, have been dismissed, and I hear from them no more. Even the tried friend of my childhood, Madame Soubise, I have been constrained to dismiss. Where are now the men of piety, learning, and probity, who a few years since made my court one of the most brilliant in Europe? Where is Perigrino Morata? Thank heaven, he died before the persecution began. Where are Celio Curione, Bartolomeo Ricci, Chilian and Jean Sinapi, Antonio Flaminio, and many others on whose wisdom and fidelity I could rely? Are they not all dead or banished? Fannio of Faenza, Giorgio Siculo, and many others, have testified their faith in the piazza, and after passing through the hands of the executioner, received the crown of martyrdom. Those of the faithful and learned in other countries, who guided me with their wise advice, and encouraged me to maintain the faith and defend its professors, have now ceased to correspond with me. From Melancthon and Farel, who formerly addressed me frequently, I now no longer hear, and letters from my friend John Calvin are of very rare occurrence. All on whom I relied are either dead or seem to have deserted me in my trouble. Your father, Teresa, is the only friend I have to guide me, and he is able to give me but little aid."

"Excuse me, your Highness," said

Teresa, who not only bore a profound love for her father, but unlimited respect for his wisdom and sagacity, "but I hardly think you do my father justice. There are few more learned men in Ferrara than he is, few more ardent in the Protestant cause, or more devoted to your Highness."

"All that I admit, my child," said Renée. "But at the same time your father, from his position, as an upright judge, is impeded from offering me all the support he might do, lest he should put himself in opposition to the laws he is bound to administer with justice."

Renée now rose from her chair, and for some moments paced the room to and fro in deep affliction, her attendants the while maintaining an absolute silence. Presently she stopped, and wiping the tears from her eyes, said :—

"But this is not the time for me to give way without a struggle while I have one under my roof who has confided himself to me for protection, nor shall he fail to receive it as long as I can lift a finger or exercise a thought in his defence. One thing is certain, he must abide with us no longer than we can insure his escape with safety. I think you told me, Teresa, that your father had already taken steps for him to leave Ferrara ?"

" He has, your Highness ; but I am not certain whether they are all completely determined on, although I believe they are."

" At any rate," said the Duchess, " our better plan will be to talk the matter coolly over with him, so that we may hear what his wishes are on the subject, and, as far as they are consistent with his safety, carry them out. It is now more than ever imperative that his residence here should be kept a secret from all. To avoid any accident, you had better go, Teresa, to the apartments of the Princesses, and tell them I will excuse their attendance this afternoon ; and you, Ponte, go to the

apartments of the Pastor Ochino, and inform him I much wish to speak to him;
and we shall then at our leisure be able to
talk over his position with him. When
you return, we will meet in my private
sitting-room, where we can converse together without fear of being interrupted."

Teresa now left the room and proceeded
to the apartments of the Princesses. On
entering she found them in company with
Sister Laura the nun, Madonna Bonifazio,
and the Jesuit Pelletario. The Princesses
no sooner saw their young friend than they
rose from their chairs to meet her, and
kissed her affectionately. Perceiving from
the redness of her eyes that she had been
weeping, the Princess Lucrezia asked her
whether anything had occurred to make
her unhappy. Teresa replied somewhat
evasively that she felt very low-spirited,
but she hoped it would soon pass off. The
two Princesses looked at each other as if
they were hardly satisfied with Teresa's

answer, but they made no further remark on the subject. Sister Laura and Madonna Bonifazio also advanced to meet her, and received her in a most friendly manner, while the Jesuit spoke to her with great blandness and courtesy, not unmixed with kindness in his tone.

"I suppose you have come," said the Princess Eleanora to her, "to tell us that her Highness is ready to receive us?"

"Pardon me," said Teresa, "her Highness, on the contrary, has requested me to tell you that as she does not feel in good spirits this afternoon, nor altogether in good health, she will dispense with your visit. At the same time, she requests me to convey to you the assurance of the warm love she bears you, and her regret at not being able to receive you."

An expression of astonishment was now visible on the faces of the Princesses, as well as on those of Madonna Bonifazio and the nun, and they looked at one another in an inquiring manner, as if convinced there was some other cause than the one Teresa had named. Even the Jesuit Pelletario seemed somewhat to have lost his habitual command of feature, as his face now assumed an expression of sorrow when he heard the Duchess was indisposed, mingled with a thoughtfulness which showed he understood there was something concealed, and he was reflecting deeply what it might be.

"But, Teresa," said the Princess Eleanora, "have you told us the whole truth? Surely her Highness is not more unwell than you would allow us to imagine? These are not times, with the plague already appearing in Ferrara, for us to hear of the illness of our dear mother without wishing to know fully what ails her. You are not deceiving us, dear Teresa, by way of calming our fears?"

"No, I assure you," said Teresa. "The bodily illness of her Highness is of the most trifling description; in fact, it would perhaps have been better for me to have said fatigue rather than illness."

" Has her Highness then left the Palace this morning," inquired Madonna Bonifazio, " and over-fatigued herself ?"

" No," said Teresa, stammering ; " her Highness has not left the Palace."

" Come, dear Teresa," said the Princess Lucrezia, " tell us the truth."

" Well," said Teresa, now fairly at bay, " the Duchess has received this morning an unexpected and very long visit, and she feels somewhat fatigued by it."

" A visit! and from whom ?"

It was impossible for Teresa to escape this explicit question, and she replied—

" It was from a Dominican monk, sent by his Majesty the King of France, on a message to her Highness. He arrived in Ferrara only yesterday."

" Do you know his name ?" asked Sister Laura, with much interest in her tone.

" Oriz."

" And what did he want with our mother?" said the Princess Eleanora. " What message could he bring her?"

Teresa now coloured deeply, and attempted to stammer out some excuse for not answering the question, but this she did in so confused and artificial a manner, as greatly to excite the curiosity of the Princesses and their two companions. Teresa, noticing their surprise, became even more confused, and an awkward silence of some moments ensued, which was broken by the Jesuit Pelletario, who during the conversation between Teresa and the Princesses had remained at some distance, apparently absorbed in thought, though marking attentively the embarrassment of the young girl, and doubtless drawing his own conclusions from it.

" Possibly," he said in his blandest tones, as he advanced towards the group, " it

would be indiscreet to ask the object of the
Reverend Father's visit to her Highness,
even if your friend Teresa had been present
at it. She may very naturally consider
herself—and in my opinion if she does she
has reason on her side—hardly authorized
to speak on the subject without permission
from her Highness. I think, if you will
allow me to suggest it, it would perhaps be
more discreet if we did not question her
further in the matter."

Teresa made no remark, but merely
bowed as if she admitted the correctness of
the Jesuit's conclusion; but notwithstanding he had relieved her from a difficult
position, she hardly felt grateful to him, for
she was but ill at ease in his presence, and
yet he had done nothing to excite either her
suspicion or her anxiety. Although he had
treated her with his habitual courtesy, and
had turned his eye from her shortly after
she had entered the room, and appeared
occupied with his own thoughts, she in-

stinctively felt that he was paying marked
attention to the conversation. On the few
occasions when his eyes were bent upon
her there was nothing in their expression
but kindness and courtesy. Still the young
girl felt that at that very moment he was
reading her inmost thoughts, and that too
in direct opposition to her own wish.
Although not an idea had crossed her mind
save of the most ingenuous and honourable
description, the certainty that the suave,
polished man who stood before her could
read her with perfect facility, occasioned in
her an intolerably painful consciousness of
her own mental inferiority. Annoyed with
herself at giving way to the feeling, the
poor girl stammered out some excuse about
the Duchess requiring her presence, and
asked permission to leave the room.
Possibly this might not have been granted
so readily, for the curiosity of the Princesses was but barely satisfied, had it not
been for the intervention of the Jesuit, who

suggested that, as her Highness the Duchess required Teresa's presence, it would hardly be respectful on their part to detain her, pleasing though her society might be to them. A glance, this time almost of gratitude, Teresa cast on the Jesuit, and then saluting the Princesses and their companions, she quitted the room.

A moment after Teresa had entered the private apartments of the Duchess, Ochino, accompanied by Madonna Ponte, followed her. The Duchess welcomed him most graciously. She then informed him in detail of the visit she had that morning received from Oriz, and the conversation which had passed between them. Ochino seemed greatly surprised at the intelligence.

" Alas! this is terrible news indeed for the faithful in Ferrara," he said. " Mercy is unknown to that man, and unfortunately his cruelty is combined with a cunning and sagacity which renders it still more terrible. However, we are in the hands of the

Almighty, and we must submit with resignation to His fiat."

"But while our lives are as naught in the balance," said Renée, "yours is very precious to the cause of Truth: and the first object of our thoughts must be to provide for your welfare. Willingly would I have asked you to remain longer with us, but I can foresee as clearly as you do the terrible danger we are all in. The sooner you quit Ferrara the greater will be your chance of reaching Venice in safety. Preparations are already in progress to obtain a boat by which you may drop down the river in safety to Commacchio, where you can easily find a vessel which shall convey you to Venice, unless you prefer returning across the Alps to Zurich."

"I should prefer first visiting Venice, your Highness," said Ochino. "There I have friends to protect me, and there, as I told you before, I am certain of receiving rich contributions for my mission in Zurich.

I will obey the suggestion of your Highness, and quit Ferrara as soon as I possibly can, to make preparations for receiving those of our faith who, I can easily perceive, will shortly be obliged to leave the duchy. At the same time, if your Highness will permit it, I should much like to have another meeting of the faithful before I quit the city, in order that I may, to the best of my ability, encourage those who may be likely to swerve from the right way as soon as the persecutions, which will shortly be in store for them shall fall heavily upon them."

"I would willingly oblige you," said Renée, "if it were practicable, but I hardly think it will be so. To-morrow night at the latest, you must leave Ferrara, and to collect the faithful together in my private chapel this evening will, I am afraid, be impossible. I have no doubt, however, that some few of us will be able to assemble together, and I will get Teresa to go to her father's with Madonna Ponte, and ask him to enlist the services of the young Swiss in collecting together what few of our faith he can before the evening, though it is now so late in the afternoon that I am afraid not many of those who last heard you will be present at this meeting."

The conversation now turned on Ochino's mission in Zurich, and his prospect of success. He detailed to the Duchess the different arrangments he had made for the reception of any fresh fugitives who might fly there for shelter. The Duchess then made many inquiries respecting different members of the Protestant faith who had already fled from Ferrara, and among them a certain Luigia Berenetti and her son, in whom she had taken great interest, supplying them with funds for their escape. Ochino did not remember their name as being among those fugitives who had assembled at Zurich.

" You surprise me," said Renée, " as she told me, when leaving, that she intended to reside for the future in Zurich. She is a woman of very modest and retiring disposition, and very possibly has not introduced herself to you, or she may not have arrived there till after you left. I much regret, however, that you have not seen her, as I feel great interest in her.

"I am by no means certain that she may not be with us," said Ochino; "for shortly before I quitted Zurich several Italians joined us, and she might have been among the number, though I have forgotten her name. I have with me a list of all our congregation, and if your Highness will permit me, I will fetch it from my room, and I shall then be able to give you more accurate information on the subject."

Ochino now proceeded to his own chamber when, having obtained the list, he descended the staircase, and entering the corridor, he found himself face to face with the Jesuit Pelletario. Recognising each other, both stopped short, and for some moments

silent looks passed between them. Pelletario at last said with much sorrow in his
tone—

"I am grieved, my brother, to find you
here, as it places me in a most painful position, and the more so from the vivid
remembrance of the friendship which once
existed between us. Warm as that was,
and painful as it undoubtedly is for me to
take any steps against you, I cannot allow a
private feeling of my own to interfere with
my duty either to our holy cause or to his
Highness."

"You intend to denounce me then?" said
Ochino.

"Candidly, I do. I have unfortunately, as
you yourself must admit, no alternative.
*To-morrow* it will be my painful duty to
inform the Duke that you are residing in
the Palace. I should have done so this evening, but that I understand his Highness has
left the castle to pass the night in either the
Belfiore or the Belvedere Palace, I know

not which. He will return, however, to the
castle to-morrow. I am in doubt whether
it is not my duty at once to inform the
Holy Office that you are in Ferrara, and I
should do so without a moment's hesitation
but that you are the guest of her Highness;
and I am not certain whether, out of respect
to the Duke, I ought not in the first place,
to put the matter into his hands. Once
more, believe me I shall do so with great
sorrow, but, as I said before, my personal
feelings must not interfere with my duty."

So saying, he courteously bowed his head
to Ochino, and without saying another
word, passed on towards the apartment of
the Princesses.

Although the literal meaning of the
words Pelletario uttered showed but little
good feeling towards Ochino, there was at
the same time considerable kindness noticeable in his tone, as well as an expression of
much sympathy on his handsome and intelligent features. Not only was there a

sorrowful accent in his words, but he spoke
them with remarkable slowness, glancing
at Ochino the while with a peculiar expression, as if wishing to obtain his particular
attention. Moreover, on the word "to-
morrow" he laid a strong emphasis, as if
wishing to convey a meaning beyond that
of the word itself. After a moment's reflection, it became evident to Ochino that there
was more of a friendly intention towards
him in Pelletario's address than might have
been at first apparent from the words he
uttered. Altogether it seemed as if he
wished to give his old friend an opportunity
of making his escape that evening. At any
rate, Ochino understood it so, and determined if possible to profit by the suggestion.

When Ochino entered the private sitting-
room of the Duchess, it was easy to perceive
that he had some unpleasant intelligence to
communicate. Before the Duchess could
question him on the subject, he narrated to

her the short interview which had passed between him and the Jesuit.

At first Renée appeared indignant that Pelletario had intruded himself in the portion of the Palace where Ochino had met him.

"His instructions," said Renée, "were to confine himself solely to the apartments of the Princesses, nor will I allow him to intrude himself beyond. All the dominion now left me to rule over is but one portion of this Palace; but that portion shall remain inviolable as long as I have the power to maintain it."

"Pardon me," said Ochino, "if I submit that possibly in disobeying the regulation which prohibited him from visiting your portion of the Palace, he might have been actuated to a certain extent by a friendly feeling towards me. Although it is perfectly true, that in the words he uttered, not one of good feeling could be detected, yet at the same time there was much kindness in his tone and manner. He evidently wished, as I believe, to impress upon me the necessity there was of my escaping, if possible, this evening. Whether it would be worth while for me to attempt it is another matter; for broken spirited as I am from the dangers surrounding our brethren in this city, were I to follow my own impulse, I should prefer staying to die with them to escaping without them."

"That must not be," said Renée. "Your life is too valuable to our cause for it to be needlessly sacrificed. But now remains the difficult question—how, at so short a notice, can we provide for your escape? To remain here till to-morrow will bring on you certain destruction; and yet it is very doubtful whether before to-morrow evening it will be possible to make the necessary preparations. Your better plan will be to remain with us till after nightfall, and then to seek the dwelling of the Judge Biagio Rosetti. Tell him the position in which you are placed, and ask

15—2

shelter from him till to-morrow. Do you not think that will be best, Teresa?" she continued, turning to the young girl.

"I can suggest no better plan," said Teresa; "and I need hardly say that my father will receive him with open arms, and do everything in his power to assist him to escape. You know where my father lives?" she continued turning to Ochino.

"Perfectly well. I know every street in Ferrara, and shall be able to find my way to his house without the slightest difficulty. I have no doubt the agents of the Inquisition will seek for me here to-morrow, as soon as Pelletario shall have given the Duke notice that I am in Ferrara. Not a word must therefore be said to lead to the place of my concealment; for although I care but little for myself in the matter, it may bring misfortune on the head of your excellent father. Again, it is more than probable he may find for me some other place of concealment, as suspicion will naturally turn on him when it is found that I am not in the Palace."

"I have no doubt," said Teresa, "that my father will ask for the assistance of the Swiss, Camille Gurdon, whom you saw here, and will confide to him the means for contriving your escape, as he will not only be more energetic but less likely to be suspected than my father. I feel quite hopeful that, once under his care, your escape will be effected with little difficulty, for he is not only shrewd and cautious, but resolute and energetic. At least, so my father thinks," she continued.

"You will indeed be in good hands if you intrust yourself to him," said Renée. "And now that we have so far determined on the course to be pursued, let us talk of other things. Teresa, my child, go to the oak chest beside my bed, and take from it the small box in which I keep some of my jewels, and bring it to me."

Teresa obeyed, and going into the bed-chamber, opened the lid of the heavy carved oak chest, with its ponderous lock, in which the ladies in Italy, in Renée's time, were accustomed to keep their richer dresses and valuables. From it she took a small silver casket exquisitely chased by Benvenuto Cellini for the late Duchess Lucrezia Borgia, and which, on Renée's marriage with her son, the reigning Duke, had been presented to her by his father Alfonso, together with many of the rich jewels Lucrezia had worn.

Teresa carried the casket to the Duchess, who, opening the secret spring which fastened it, took from it a purse containing a number of sequins and a diamond armlet of great value (one of the jewels of the late Duchess), and placing them in Ochino's hand, she begged he would, when in Venice, exchange the latter into money, and apply the proceeds as well as the purse of sequins to the uses of the mission in Zurich. Ochino received the contribution most thankfully, and reminded her of the text, "He that hath pity upon the poor, lendeth unto the Lord," and told her that without doubt her gift would be repaid to her a hundred-fold. He now proposed that they should spend the remainder of the evening, till it was time for him to depart, in prayer. Willingly the Duchess agreed to the proposition, and Teresa having been despatched to the chapel for the Italian translation of the Scriptures, Ochino read a portion of the New Testament. Then, all kneeling down, he prayed with great fervour, begging that the bounty and protection of the Almighty might be bestowed, not only on the Duchess and her suite, but on the suffering members of Christ's flock, dispersed in Ferrara and throughout the whole duchy. That courage and patience might be given them to support the persecutions which were too probably in store for them, and to enable them to maintain the faith even under the tortures of the rack, in the dungeons of the Inquisition, or amid the flames on the Piazza. That God would raise up for them wise counsellors, who would be able to guide and protect them in their adversity, and support them with His Spirit till the day should arrive when truth should be made manifest among them, and the sword of the persecutor drop from his hand.

It was dark night when Ochino had concluded his devotions. After a sorrowful leave-taking with the Duchess, Teresa, carrying a small lamp in her hand, conducted him stealthily downstairs to a private door of the Palace, and, having ascertained that no loiterers were in sight, bade him farewell.

# CHAPTER XI.

## THE CONFERENCE.

ROM an early hour the next morning all was stir and animation in the convent of the Corpus Domini. In consequence of Renée's frank admission to Oriz, that she had adopted the Reformed doctrines, and had expressed her determination to continue in them, the Superior of the Dominicans the same evening had sent messages not only to the Archbishops and Bishops of Ferrara, and the heads of the regular clergy, but to the Superiors of the different monastic institutions, requesting their attendance at a meeting to be held the next day in the refectory of the Dominican convent, to take into consideration the best means to be adopted at once to put a stop to the baneful heresy which now afflicted the Church in the Duchies of Ferrara and Modena. The message also stated that another object of the meeting was to receive the Reverend Dr. Matthew Oriz, Chief Inquisitor of France, who had been sent by the Most Christian King Henry II. on a special mission to the Duchy.

By nine o'clock, the refectory had been put in perfect order for the meeting, and the lay brother in charge of the arrangements having declared all to be in readiness, the Superior of the convent and Oriz descended to inspect the preparations which had been made. After expressing their approval, the lay brother retired, and an earnest conversation ensued between the two monks—earnest at least so far as the apparently impassive nature of Oriz would allow him to show. Their conversation principally turned on the business to be presented to the meeting, and the necessity there was for impressing on it that the moment had come when energetic action should be taken. Oriz, his habitually calm eye lightening up as he spoke, expressed his opinion that now the plague of heresy in the Duchy might be extirpated at a single blow, and the Church again resume her authority. The Superior fully agreed with Oriz. In fact, the two monks seemed to have changed their relative positions, for while Oriz in his manner showed towards his companion the obedience and respect due to the Superior of a convent, in his tone he undisguisedly assumed the lead; while, again, the Superior, accepting the outward signs of respect shown him by Oriz, quietly acquiesced in every opinion he uttered, and expressed his willingness to carry out every plan of action suggested.

The first delegate to the meeting who arrived at the convent was the General of the Capuchins. This office had been twice held by Ochino when he was a brother of the Order. A strong difference, however, existed between the present General and

Ochino. While the latter was all animation, brilliant in his discourse, and graceful in his person, his successor was even common in his appearance, of heavy frame, and unintellectual countenance. His principal qualifications for the appointment he held were those of a discreet superintendent of the funds of his Order, and an attorney-like astuteness in prosecuting with success obscure points connected with the legality of pecuniary or property claims supposed to belong to the fraternity.

On being introduced to Oriz, he shortly expressed the great gratification he felt at the arrival of so eminent a man, who, he had no doubt, would contribute greatly not only to the spiritual welfare of the Church, but to her power as well. Oriz gratefully thanked the Capuchin for the compliment he had paid him, and in return trusted that he should have the General's assistance in the good work they were about to enter on.

" You may be perfectly certain," said the

General, "that all the assistance in my power, and in that of the brethren of our Order, shall be willingly rendered you, and I flatter myself you will find us energetic soldiers of the Church."

"At the same time," said Oriz, "the Church not only requires brave soldiers, but disciplined ones as well. Without discipline one half our power will be lost. We have already reformed the plan of action of the Holy Office, and we trust that all will assist us by putting into our hands whatever information may come under their notice. Not that we doubt the discretion or ability of others, yet, at the same time, one central authority is necessary, and by permission of our Holy Father the Pope, that is at present placed in our hands; so that by accumulating all kinds of information, we may be better able to strike the blow where it will be most effective."

"I perfectly agree with you," said the Capuchin General; "and I moreover hold that no information, of however trifling a description, should be kept from you; and in proof, the object of my early arrival at the convent was to place in your hands some information, possibly trifling in itself, which reached me yesterday. In the morning, an old man of the name of Carlo Pedretti, formerly employed to strike the hours in the Rigobello tower, called at our convent, to inquire after a brother whom he had brought with him into the city two nights before, but whom he had parted with before reaching the convent. On inquiring among the brethren, no one was found answering to the description. The old man was told he was in error, as all the brethren had been at the benediction in the convent that evening, and no one had afterwards quitted the building. The old man, however, insisted that he was not in error, stating that he had rowed a travelling Capuchin across the river long after Ave Maria, as the regular ferry-boats were

not allowed to work later. In vain was
he assured that no travelling brother had
arrived at the convent on the evening in
question. Pedretti maintained that it was
the case, and that he had conducted him
nearly to the corner of the street. On
being required to give a description of the
Friar, he replied that he had not seen his
features, for besides that it was nearly dark
when he first addressed him, he now remembered that he wore his cowl deep over
his face, a fact which he did not remark at
the time, but which afterwards had recurred
to his memory more than once. On being
asked what object he had in visiting the
the new-comer, he replied with some hesitation, that he had no particular reason
beyond being somewhat uneasy in his conscience, for although nothing extraordinary
had struck him at the time in the Friar's
behaviour, there had ever since appeared
to him to be some mystery about it. In
the first place, he did not clearly under-

stand why he should have objected to enter
the city by the Via del Po. The Porta
del Po was not at so great a distance from
the Capuchin convent as to have induced
the friar to wade a mile through the clay
and marshes when it was nearly dark, and
when it was uncertain whether he would
be able to get ferried over, especially when
he knew that without trouble he could have
obtained a place in the ferry-boat at Mal-
Albergo. He couldn't understand it, he
said. The way there would have been
quite as easy to find as by the Porta
San Giorgio; and besides that, he would
have passed by the convent of the Corpus
Domini, where he could have asked his way
if he had had any difficulty. And then
again it struck him, that in leaving the
high road and crossing the marshes, it almost seemed as if the Friar wished to visit
the heretic ferryman, Giacomo, as he was
evidently proceeding in a straight line to
his house. We questioned him," continued

the Capuchin General, "as to what could have put these doubts into his head. He replied, that on thinking over the conversation which had passed between them, he remembered that the Friar had not only defended and spoken well of the Duchess, but had also made particular inquiries whether the heretic Judge Biagio Rosetti was still in Ferrara. Altogether he had been unhappy about it ever since, and had called at the convent to get such explanation about it as might serve as a salve to his conscience. Although, of course, we did not let Pedretti see we were at all anxious on the subject, we caused inquiries to be made through the whole of the city, but no tidings could we gain of the Friar. I therefore wish to submit to you whether it may not be possible that some heretic of note has introduced himself into the city under the disguise of a member of our Holy Order."

"Nothing more likely," said the Superior of the Dominicans. "We all know the arch-heretic John Calvin himself has already more than once visited the city in disguise, to encourage in their evil ways those whom by his pernicious doctrines he had led astray. The subject shall receive the serious attention of the Holy Office, and we are most grateful to you for having brought it under our notice."

It was now nearly time for the meeting, and members of the different bodies began to arrive. Among the earliest were the Arch-bishop of Ferrara and the Jesuit Pelletario. Then came the delegates from the Carthusian monastery in the Via Borsa, attended by two brothers of the order, the Superior of the Theatins, and many members of other different religious bodies, as well as the most eminent of the parochial clergy, till the large hall of the refectory was completely filled with clergy, all anxious to take a part in the proceedings, as well as to receive the celebrated Inquisitor and doctor in theology, who was that day to be presented to them.

After many of the most notable among them had been presented to Oriz, the Archbishop of Ferrara was invited to preside, and having taken his seat in a small, slightly elevated open pulpit, which somewhat resembled the throne of a judge, with Oriz on the one side of him and the Superior of the Dominicans on the other, the rest of the meeting ranged themselves round him, the whole forming one of those picturesque combinations for which the costumes of the Roman Catholic clergy appear so peculiarly adapted.

The Archbishop now rose to address the meeting. He told them that although several among them had already formed the acquaintance of Dr. Matthew Oriz, it was now his pleasing duty to introduce him generally to the assembly. Their reverend brother, who had filled the high office of Chief Inquisitor of France, had now arrived in Ferrara on a special mission of importance from the Most Christian King, his Majesty Henry II., as well as authorized by His Holiness to take the supreme direction of the Holy Office established in the city. Of the special mission with which his reverend brother had been intrusted by his Majesty, it was not for him to speak. What the purport of his instructions might be he knew nothing, but of this he was persuaded, that, whether he divulged or kept them secret, they might all be assured that their reverend brother would be actuated by one principle — the advancement and good of the Church. Of this he could promise the reverend doctor, that whatever help he might require from the regular clergy or monastic orders in the diocese, he would be certain to receive it—all being assured that a man of his eminence, and holding as he did the important position of Chief Inquisitor of France, would ask for no aid or information which they would not willingly accord him.

A simultaneous burst of acquiescence broke from the assembly, and when it had somewhat subsided the Inquisitor Oriz rose to address the meeting. Flattering as had been the reception they had given him, it seemed not to make the slightest impression on his feelings. Not the least appearance of excitement was noticeable on his countenance, and the tone of his voice was calm and unimpassioned. He commenced by thanking them for the assistance he was convinced every individual would willingly accord him, but before asking it he should like to explain, as far as discretion would allow him, the object of his mission, and the reasons, beyond the commands of his superiors, which had induced him to undertake it.

" It was not," he said, " from any doubt of the energy or ability shown by the Dominican Fathers in Ferrara, in the management of the duties of the Holy Office, which induced his Majesty the King of France to request me to undertake the mission, as that Most Christian King would have been averse to interfere in either the ecclesiastical or political affairs of the Duchy of Ferrara. On the contrary, it was the direct request and application of his Highness the Duke himself that induced his Majesty to intrust me with the mission. In the summer of last year the Duke wrote a letter to his Majesty the King of France, in which, after speaking of the unfortunate spread of heresy in his dominions—heresy from which his own family were not altogether free— he requested his Majesty to send him an ecclesiastic well versed in argument, and accustomed to the duties of an inquisitor, who might succeed in bringing the illustrious Duchess Renée of France back into the fold of the Church, as well as assist, by his advice and experience, his brother Dominicans in extirpating the evil which had been introduced into the city by the arch-heretic John Calvin, and which has since taken such strong root in Ferrara, that it was lately pointed at by Luther himself as the centre of Protestantism in Italy. Fortunately, through the admirable energy of the reverend fathers of the Inquisition, aided by the counsel and wisdom of that true son of the Church, the reigning Duke, that unhappy state of things no longer exists. In Italy at present heresy has no rallying point, nor can Ferrara be now designated as the stronghold of schismatics; for although there are still many deluded ones resident in the city, they are as sheep without a shepherd. Already heresy is nearly extinct in the valley of Aosta, that district which Calvin considered exclusively his own. In Como hardly a heretic remains; and the schismatic Churches of Pisa, Florence, and Naples are either extinct or their deluded members meet secretly to perform a worship scarcely less obnoxious to our Church than the worship of the arch-fiend himself. In Venice, notwithstanding the headstrong opposition of the senate, and their determination not to allow the ecclesiastical law, which should rule all laws, to be dominant over the civil power, the true religion is regaining her sway. Still the heretics in all parts, deceived by their priesthood, look to Ferrara as a rallying-point, and believe they will yet receive support and protection from the illustrious Duchess, who has now, under the blessing of heaven, lost all her power to do evil. From this idea it will be our duty to undeceive them. We must prove to them that Ferrara is no longer the hotbed of schism it was when Ochino openly defied the powers of Rome, and the arch-heretic Calvin (though under an assumed name) boldly opened a school for the dissemination of his schismatic doctrines under the protection of the Duchess herself, and openly preached defiance of the Pope,

hurling his blasphemous denunciations at
what he termed the idolatry of the mass,
that most respected and beloved of the
mysteries of our Church. All this, we
must shortly prove to the whole of Italy,
is a thing of the past. Although it is
certain there are many in Ferrara who
still cling with determined tenacity to the
depraved doctrines of the so-called Reformers, there can be no doubt that a
divine blessing has now fallen on the
labours of the holy Inquisition, and that
in a short time Italy will be freed from
the pestilence, and the Church resume
again her original power and splendour."

Although during the greater part of his
address, which lasted nearly an hour, Oriz
maintained his usual calm tone and manner,
his words falling slowly and impressively
on the ear, when he spoke of the hope he
felt that the Church would soon again be
dominant, his manner suddenly changed so
completely, that he could hardly have been

recognised as the same individual. He had stood till then with his body slightly bent, keeping his eyes on the floor of the hall, occasionally, and only for a moment, raising them when he personally addressed the Archbishop, and then lowering them again when he resumed the thread of his subject. But when he touched on the future glorious prospect of the Church he drew himself up to his full height, and with wonderful animation gazed on the assembled priests and monks, his voice assuming at the time such power of tone and fluency of diction as to make him appear almost inspired. At the conclusion of his address, however, the brilliant animation which had sparkled in his eye suddenly vanished, and the flush which had at the moment overspread his countenance disappeared, leaving the same marble hue which his complexion had worn before he commenced speaking. Again assuming his habitual calm demeanour, and bowing humbly and almost deprecatingly to the buzz of admiration which spontaneously burst from the assembly, he withdrew from his prominent position beside the Archbishop, and retired to one of the back seats, as if the congratulations and applause he was receiving were painful to him.

The Father Fabrizio, the Superior of the convent of the Dominicans, now rose to address the meeting. He said that although he wished to resign his office as Superior of the convent, the Reverend Father Oriz would not allow him. He much regretted the fact, as in his humble opinion the interests of the Church would have been advanced by it. At the same time it was his duty not to put his wish in opposition to one so far more learned than himself. It was his part to obey, and he would do so. He could not disguise from himself that it would be detrimental to the interests of the Church, and an act of presumption on his part, if he continued longer as the head of

the executive of the Holy Office in extirpating the remains of heresy in Ferrara. For
the future that labour would be put into
the hands of the Reverend Dr. Oriz, and
he (the Superior) would, in all subjects
connected with the Holy Office, act as his
subordinate. He flattered himself that
although the secular power had latterly
been but little used in Ferrara, the reverend
Father would find that he had not been idle.
True, they had occasionally employed the
secular power, and punished in an exem-
plary manner many of those who, after due
admonition, had been found obstinate in
their heresy, or had relapsed. They had
done so the rather as examples and warn-
ings to others, as well as to show that the
Fathers of the Holy Office were not sleep-
ing at their posts. But while the outward
demonstrations of energetic action were
perhaps less visible in Ferrara than in many
other towns in Italy where the foul heresy
of Lutheranism or Calvinism had taken root,

they should be fully able to prove to the reverend Father that they had been actively employed the while, and were totally free from any charge of lukewarmness. Anticipating the arrival of the reverend Inquisitor of the faith, they had lately principally occupied themselves in obtaining information as to the spread of heresy in the Duchy, and what were the numbers and position in life of those infected by it; and so well had they succeeded that at the present moment he could confidently state they were ripe for action. They had now but to place the reins of power in the hands of their reverend brother, and no doubt in a short time there would not be a city in Italy clearer from the stain of heresy than Ferrara.

Several other speakers followed the Superior of the Dominicans, and among them a monk of the Carthusian Order, whose convent was at Modena, but who had now arrived at Ferrara for the purpose of giving the Holy Office a description of the state of the Church in his city. After expressing his great satisfaction at having heard the address, and personally making the acquaintance of the Reverend Dr. Matthew Oriz, of whose reputation as a true soldier of the Church all Christian Europe was well aware, he proceeded to describe the condition of the heretics in the sister city of Modena, and the exertions made by the clergy—especially the monastic orders—to extirpate heresy. He regretted to state that Modena was scarcely less infected than Ferrara itself. In the latter city the populace had been misled by many teachers of eminence and ability, who had not only infected the learned, but obtained their assistance in disseminating the pernicious doctrines they taught. The mass of the populace, unable to understand the sophistry made use of, yet respecting those more learned than themselves, had adopted those doctrines without attempting to understand the fallacious arguments brought forward to support them. In Modena, on the contrary, the Calvinists were, as a rule, of a far less educated class than in Ferrara, and less likely to offer any effectual opposition to the power of the Inquisition. At present, as in Ferrara, the clergy of Modena had for some time past been openly less energetic in their punishment of offenders, but they had in the meantime made themselves thoroughly acquainted with the names, opinions, and ability of those professing heretical doctrines; and they now only waited for the example of Ferrara, to strike one last powerful blow that should put an end to schism in the city.

A monk from Commacchio next spoke, who described the state of that town as strongly resembling Modena. Several others followed, all of whom agreed that the time had now arrived for energetic action, and that shortly there would not be found in the whole of the Duchy an individual who was not a true son of the Church of Rome.

The meeting now broke up, and for some time conversation on the state of the Church and matters relating to ecclesiastical affairs was carried on among the members, who stood in groups till the bell tolled for mass, and the whole assembly then forming themselves into a procession, entered the magnificent church of the Corpus Domini, attached to the convent, where mass was performed with great pomp by the Archbishop. When it was concluded, the principal doors, which had been closed during the ceremony, were opened to allow the congregation to leave the church. But here an unexpected obstacle presented itself to their quiet departure. In the open space before the church an immense crowd had collected, their curiosity having been raised by the large number of ecclesiastics they had seen enter the monastery. Indeed, judging that some ceremony of unusual magnificence was likely to be performed in the church, they had assembled to witness it. They were, however, doomed to be disappointed, for the sacristans having received notice that the mass would be strictly private, the only persons allowed to be present being ecclesiastics and members of the different orders of monks, the great doors were closed, much to the annoyance of the populace who wished to assist at it. Even when the doors were opened, many rushed forward, anxious to enter the building, and the sacristans and lay-brothers at first experienced much trouble in stopping them. In a short time, however, order was completely restored. The venerable Archbishop advanced to the door, followed by the rest of the assembly, with the exception of the Jesuit Pelletario, who remained performing some devotions at one of the altars. As soon as the Archbishop was recognised all disorder subsided, and the assembled crowd, after leaving a space for him and those that followed to walk through, devoutly knelt to receive his blessing as he passed. He continued his way onward, bestowing his benediction on them as he went, till he had reached the street leading to the castle, when he entered the litter in which he had arrived at the convent. Those of the clergy who had followed then dispersed to their different homes, and in a short time the excitement which the meeting had caused among the populace completely subsided.

# CHAPTER XII.

## THE TRIAL OF STRENGTH.

THE Jesuit Pelletario, having been invited to attend the meeting of ecclesiastics to be held in the refectory of the convent of the Corpus Domini, left the Palace of San Francesco an hour before the time appointed, for the purpose of first calling at the castle to ascertain whether the Duke had returned to it, and probably, as he had threatened, to inform his Highness that Ochino was then a guest of the Duchess. On arriving at the Gate of the Lions, the sentinel on duty immediately recognised him, and calling to the officer on guard at the inner gate, the drawbridge was lowered to allow him to enter. The officer

17—2

received the Duke's confessor with great
respect, and begged permission to kiss his
hand, which Pelletario allowed him to do,
and he then asked if his Highness had returned to the castle.

"He returned at a late hour yesterday
evening, Reverend Father," was the officer's
reply.

"Is he here now?"

"He is; but I heard it rumoured that his
Highness intends leaving Ferrara this afternoon to visit Belriguardo. How far this is
correct I know not; but doubtless the
major-domo will be able to give you more
accurate information on the subject. Is
there anything further I can do to serve
you, Reverend Father?"

"Nothing at present, I thank you," said
Pelletario, and saluting condescendingly
those who had gathered around him, he left
the gate and proceeded up the grand staircase to the landing, where he met the major-
domo at the doorway leading into the great

hall. By this official Pelletario was received with even greater demonstrations of respect than had been shown him by the officer on guard at the drawbridge. To his inquiry in what way he could serve him, Pelletario merely replied by asking if his Highness had left his private apartments.

"He has, Reverend Father," was the major-domo's answer. "He is now deeply occupied in his cabinet with two noblemen, with whom he had made an appointment. Indeed, he gave orders that no one was to disturb him; but doubtless he would make an exception in your case. Shall I inform him you wish to see him?"

At first the Jesuit appeared somewhat undecided what answer to make; but at length he said, "Is it true that his Highness intends to leave Ferrara to-day to visit Belriguardo?"

"It is."

"At what time does he propose leaving?"

"Up to the present moment I have received no precise orders on the subject, beyond that I am to see everything is in readiness for his departure. I am, however, certain he will not leave before the afternoon."

"Why not?"

"Because his Highness has made an appointment to receive at noon the reverend Dominican, Father Oriz."

Pelletario heard this intelligence with considerable surprise. He remained for some moments silent, and then said,—

"Do you know whether the appointment was made at the request of the Duke, or was it asked for by the reverend Father?"

"At the request of the reverend Father. Yesterday evening he sent a lay-brother to inquire whether his Highness had arrived; and on being told that he was not expected till late at night, he went back to the convent, and this morning early—in fact, before the Duke had risen from his bed—the same lay-brother returned, and waited till I had an opportunity to deliver his message, to which the Duke replied that he would receive the reverend Father at noon. But shall I tell his Highness you wish to see him ?"

" No," said Pelletario, " I will not disturb him now, for no doubt he is occupied on business of importance. I will return later."

So saying, the Jesuit took leave of the major-domo, and descending the staircase, quitted the castle.

The pace of Pelletario on his way to the convent was slow and deliberate in the extreme, and an expression of deep thought was on his face. So pre-occupied was he that he took but little notice of the respectful salutations he received from those he met on the road, an omission the more remarkable on his part, as he was habitually courteous and condescending to all. Nor was he without cause for his pre-occupation. As father-confessor to the Duke, his position was one of the most influential in the state, and he was universally courted and flattered. Hitherto he had been without a rival, but was that likely to continue? From the regular clergy and monastic orders in the city he had little cause for anxiety, but his mind was by no means clear with regard to Oriz. True, he only knew him by reputation, but fame spoke of him as a man of great ability, much liked by the monarchs of Spain and France. Besides, he had great confidence placed in him by his Holiness. To have arrived at such eminence he calculated must have required something more than profound theological learning and great energy in the cause of the Roman Catholic religion. He must also be possessed of that valuable qualification—the power to make himself liked by the princes of the earth, and if he had already succeeded so well with others, might he not be equally successful with the Duke? True, Oriz had not succeeded at his interview with the Duchess, but he (Pelletario) had also been unable to convince her. One difference, however, he could discover between his own interview with Renée, and that of Oriz. Although she had positively refused to listen to his arguments, he parted from her without any display of anger on her part, while she had evidently been greatly offended with Oriz; and Renée was not of a disposition easily to forget a personal affront. At the same time the Jesuit could not help admitting that the very energy of the Dominican which had caused so much anger in the breast of the Duchess might have a contrary effect with her husband. All things considered, Pelletario could not disguise from himself that his power and position were at the moment in jeopardy, and that it behoved him to play his part with great caution. To be the better able to do this, he determined, if possible, to have a trial of strength that day with the Inquisitor, and judge by the result whether he had as formidable an

adversary to deal with as at first sight
appeared probable.

It will be remembered that when the
mass terminated, and the assembly of
divines quitted the church, Pelletario alone
remained performing some devotional act
before one of the altars. This, however,
ended shortly after the church was cleared.
Then rising from his knees, he requested
the sacristan to allow him to pass by the
private way which led from the church into
the convent, as he wished to have an interview with the Reverend Doctor Oriz. The
sacristan—to whom, of course, Pelletario
was well-known — with profound respect,
not only conducted him through the private door leading into the convent, but was
on the point of accompanying him across
the quadrangle to the cell occupied by Oriz,
when the latter was seen descending the
staircase, with his head covered, and evidently on the point of leaving the
building.

Pelletario, having dismissed the sacristan, now advanced towards the Dominican.

"Pardon my interrupting you," he said, "but I was loth to return to the Palace without first complimenting you on your admirable address to the meeting this morning. Had our Church possessed a few more advocates with your ability and energy, the lamentable schism which has afflicted Christendom would never have taken the deep root it has. At the same time we have reason to be thankful that at last one has sprung up amongst us who will crush with his heel the head of the serpent which hitherto has remained with comparative impunity in the city."

"You do me too much honour," said Oriz, humbly; "or, if I have shown any of the energy or ability for which you compliment me, I am indebted to a far higher power than my own talent or inspiration."

"At least, you must admit," said Pelletario, "that if I am in error, I am not alone in it, and the manner in which the whole assembly of divines hailed the idea that you were about to assume the direction of the Inquisition in Ferrara proves it."

"Still, it might rather be attributed to their kind feeling than to my merits," said Oriz. "Yet flattering as their reception was, it rather pained than pleased me, as it seemed to convey the idea, that our reverend brother, the Superior of the convent, had not, in their estimation, conducted the affairs of the Holy Office with sufficient energy. With such a view I by no means agree. He has had great difficulties to contend with; more so than usually falls to the lot of our office, in the opposition shown him by her Highness the Duchess. On the whole, I consider he has conducted the duties of the Holy Office with great discretion and ability."

"I perfectly agree with you," said Pelletario, "in the opinion you have formed of the ability and energy of our reverend brother, the Superior of the convent, and I am much pleased to hear the kind view you take of his conduct. But, pardon me," he continued, looking on the sun-dial at the wall, " for detaining you, for I perceive you are about to quit the convent. I wish to visit his Highness to-day at noon; so, unless you are going my way, I will bid you good morning."

" It is my intention likewise to call upon his Highness," said Oriz; " in fact, I have received his commands to do so."

" If I should not be disturbing your meditations, or appear indiscreet," said Pelletario, " I should much like to accompany you."

The Dominican having expressed the pleasure he should feel in Pelletario's society, the two monks quitted the convent together.

As the time that would elapse in passing from the Dominican convent to the castle, at even the ordinary slow and deliberate pace usually maintained by ecclesiastics, would scarcely exceed a quarter of an hour, Pelletario easily perceived he had but little time to lose in his trial of strength with the Dominican, and without further delay he commenced operations.

"If I may be allowed to put a question of the kind," he said to Oriz, "is your interview with the Duke on a subject of private or public importance?"

"I hardly know, my brother, how to answer your question," said Oriz, after a moment's hesitation. "Pray be more explicit."

"My sole reason for inquiring," said Pelletario, "is, that if it were upon a subject solely of public interest connected with the Holy Office, without anything confidential being mixed with it, I thought perhaps I might be able to assist you with some information which I, perhaps erroneously, think important."

"Many thanks for the offer," said Oriz. "It is in connexion with the affairs of the Holy Office that I have requested this interview with his Highness. But, candidly, no inconsiderable portion of it is of a kind which, at first at any rate, should only meet the private ear of the Duke. At the same time, understand me, I shall, in the interests of our holy cause, be most grateful to you for any information you may give me."

"The subject on which I was about to speak to you," said Pelletario, "is one which not only regards the Holy Office, but his Highness as well. At the same time it is one of much delicacy. I should have taken upon myself to inform his Highness of it, and had called at the Palace this morning for that purpose, but as the Duke at the time was busily engaged I did not disturb him. On mature reflection, as the subject is a somewhat painful one, and coming perfectly within the duties of the Holy Office, I thought it perhaps might be better to confide it to you, that you might be the first person to inform his Highness of it."

"Anything I can do to serve his Highness, or be of use to our holy cause, I will readily attempt," said Oriz. "Might I ask to what you allude?"

Pelletario remained silent for a moment, as if hardly daring to communicate a secret of such importance even to the Inquisitor himself. At length he said, "You will hardly believe, Reverend Brother, what I am about to communicate to you, though at the same time I assure you solemnly it is a fact. That misguided man and arch-heretic, Bernardino Ochino, is at this moment in Ferrara, and a guest of her Highness the Duchess."

As Pelletario spoke this, he glanced furtively at his companion, anxious to notice the effect so weighty a communication would make on him; but not the slightest surprise or emotion was visible on the countenance of the Dominican.

"My dear brother," he replied to Pelletario, "of that fact I am well aware, and it is one of the reasons which has induced me to demand an interview with his Highness this morning."

Although the countenance of Oriz had remained impassive when Pelletario communicated to him the intelligence, not so the features of the Jesuit on hearing the Dominican's reply. The idea seemed to cross his mind whether it was not possible that the Dominican intended to profit by the discovery he (Pelletario) had made. To assure himself on this point he said to Oriz—

"Your means of obtaining information are wonderful. I should hardly have thought the organization of the Holy Office so perfect as it appears to be. Might I ask if you are aware how long Ochino has been in Ferrara?"

"Only two or three days," said Oriz. "Short, however, as the time has been, he

has already held a prayer-meeting in the
Palace of the Duchess, which was attended
by many of the heads of the schismatics."
And here Oriz not only named several of
the principal persons present on the occasion, but told Pelletario the text Ochino
had selected for his sermon, and the different arguments he had brought forward
to elucidate it.

"Do you know in what manner he contrived to enter the city?" inquired Pelletario.

"I think," said Oriz, "you were not in
the refectory before the meeting, when the
General of the Capuchins narrated to us the
adventures of an old man, who introduced
into the city late at night a stranger clad in
the frock of a Friar of their order?"

"I was not," said Pelletario.

"Because that disguised Capuchin Friar
was no other than Ochino."

"Pardon me," said Pelletario, "but are
you quite sure your information is correct?

Ochino does not wear the frock of his old order, but is dressed more in the style of a professor of the University."

"Of that I am also aware," said Oriz; "still the information of the old man was perfectly correct. The dress he now wears is one belonging to the Judge Biagio Rosetti, and the frock, the cowl, and cord in which he was disguised when he entered Ferrara, as well as the sandals he wore, are now concealed in a chest in one of the rooms in the house of the Judge."

Pellatario now made no attempt to conceal the expression of astonishment on his features at the extraordinary minuteness of the information Oriz had received. The Inquisitor, with something approaching an expression of triumph on his countenance, glanced at the astonishment stamped on the features of his companion.

"But, my brother," he continued, "all things are ordered for the best; and that wicked man will now be caught in the trap which he himself has laid, and another enemy of our Church will be crushed at the very moment when he considers himself in the most perfect security."

Oriz had turned his glance from his companion's face when he made this remark, or he might have perceived that the expression of astonishment had vanished from Pelletario's countenance and a peculiar sardonic smile occupied its place. The Jesuit said nothing, and his companion continued—

"But are there any other points you wish to communicate to me prior to my interview with his Highness? Allow me first to say that I much admire your discretion in placing the duty of communicating the intelligence to the Duke on an humble officer of the Holy Inquisition. At the same time," he continued, with something like patronage in his tone, "be assured, as soon as the first burst of indignation which naturally will arise in the mind of his Highness has somewhat subsided, I will not fail to inform him of the energy and discretion you have shown in the matter. Truly, the Duke is to be congratulated on having chosen a confessor of so much tact and experience."

The conversation continued a few minutes longer, until they reached the drawbridge, which was immediately lowered to allow them to enter ; and they passed into the great hall till the major-domo should arrive to inform them his Highness was in readiness to receive them. Little animation did Pelletario show in his tone and manner, and on being asked by Oriz if he had any further communication to make, the Jesuit told him he had not, and then added, with something like bitterness in his tone, " At least, none which I am certain is not in your possession already." Then, quitting his companion, he seemed apparently to watch the efforts of some workmen who were then occupied in terminating the repairs in that portion of the Este Palace.

At length the major-domo entered the hall, and informed the two monks that his Highness was ready to receive them; and they followed him into his presence, where they were received by the Duke with equal kindness and amiability.

" I hear you called at the Castle this morning to see me," he said to Pelletario. " I regret you did not allow the major-domo to tell me you were here. I wanted to inform you that it is my intention to leave the Castle for Belriguardo this afternoon, and I much wish you to accompany me. I trust you will be able to do so, although the notice is of the shortest."

" I shall have much pleasure in obeying the commands of your Highness," said Pelletario, with great satisfaction in his tone, for the idea at that moment had occurred to him, that he would have ample leisure when with the Duke to neutralize any ascendancy Oriz might have gained over his illustrious penitent's mind. "I will be at your service at any time you may appoint."

"I propose leaving in about an hour," said the Duke; "and I have already given orders that your mule should be in readiness for you. Will you be able to accompany me at so short a notice?"

"Certainly, your Highness," said Pelletario. "I will take my leave of you for the present, unless you have any further orders to give me."

"You can do so, if you have nothing more you wish now to say to me. If you have, I am at your service, otherwise the Reverend Father Oriz wishes for some private conversation with me."

"I will interrupt your Highness no

longer," said Pelletario. "In an hour's time I will be ready at the Castle for your departure;" and then bowing with great humility, both to the Duke and the Dominican, the Jesuit left the apartments.

END OF VOL. I.